South of the Border

James Ryan

THE LILLIPUT PRESS
DUBLIN

First published 2008 by
THE LILLIPUT PRESS
62–63 Sitric Road, Arbour Hill
Dublin 7, Ireland
www.lilliputpress.ie

ISBN 978 1 84351 140 3 (hbk)
978 1 84351 134 2 (pbk)

1 3 5 7 9 10 8 6 4 2

Set in 12 pt on 15 pt Minion by Marsha Swan
Printed in England by Athenaeum Press Ltd, Tyne and Wear

South of the Border

Chapter 1

The train chugged laboriously out of the station billowing plumes of cottony, white turf smoke. Matt Duggan, the only passenger to get off that afternoon, leaned over the hump-backed bridge, watching it disappear into the darkness below. Three miles or so across the flood plane Rathisland rose up, for all the world a submerged settlement, now mysteriously taking shape in the distance. Its church steeple craned upwards like a spindly tree searching the sky for light. A row of chimneys and high pitched roofs marked out a choppy line, boldly defining the business side of the Square, where The Royal and The Munster & Leinster Banks, as well as The Commercial Hotel were lined up as if for a military inspection. There were some houses too, double fronted homes of once quietly prosperous families, their sights now increasingly fixed on a past in which things were done differently.

Matt cupped his hand on his forehead, shielding his eyes from the late August sun. His other hand remained tightly gripped on the handle of a new, highly polished Gladstone bag, which, a few days previously, his mother had left on the chest of drawers in the room he shared with his two brothers, Hugh and Will. When, that evening, searching for a way of saying thanks, he said how swanky it looked, she was quick to reply.

'It was bought for everyone to use, but seeing as you're the one that's going away you can think of it as yours for the time being.'

Marie Duggan was embarrassed by gratitude. She was uncomfortable with the formality involved because of the distance it created between her and her sons. And there was her pride; her tight-lipped, volcanic pride that infused everything she had to say about that bag with starchy certitude, but which, in that well regulated household, had to be carefully measured in case it erupted into something uncontrollable: an outpouring of relief maybe. Or even joy that Matt, her eldest son, focus of so much hope and anxiety down the years of her widowhood, was now a qualified national school teacher, an NT with a permanent and pensionable job.

'Mr Matt Duggan NT, The Bungalow, Dublin Rd., Balbriggan, Co. Dublin', she'd written on the luggage label the evening before he was due to leave for Rathisland. Kneeling down on the hall floor, she'd gone over all the capital letters twice, making them stand out, but none more so than NT. She stepped back to examine her work, anticipating how it might appear to people in the railway station, people on the train, people everywhere. Matt's younger brother Hugh, attuned as always to the way their mother fussed over Matt, pointed at the label, 'Mr Matt Duggan NT,' he announced, flinging his hand out in Matt's direction.

'Ladies and Gentlemen, may I present a man whose genius …'

'When are you going to stop acting the clown?' Matt cut

in, well practised at positioning himself midway between his mother's coddling and the taunting it inevitably earned from his brothers. Ensuring that they all got on well together was as much a response to his father's death over a decade previously as it was to his mother's frequently voiced wish, an unrelenting demand when they were younger, for harmony in the home. 'There's no room for fighting in this house', was her catch cry, a warning that alluded to the many difficulties brought on by widowhood, implicitly raising the spectre of the boys' dead father. It was a catch cry to which all three responded, but none more so than Matt. He was not, however, uncritical of his mother. So if, for instance, he'd found himself alone with his brothers in the hall that evening, he would probably have raised his eyes at the sight of the label, prompting them to laugh at her bold statement of pride. A familiar routine would have then followed, with Hugh leading the way: 'Have you got your little rain hat?'; 'Do you need to go to the toilet?'; 'When did you last go ...?'

Care, unrelenting, self-sacrificial care, was the invisible weapon with which Marie Duggan directed the lives of her sons. So each in his own way had unwittingly accumulated a great debt of gratitude, a debt they could only repay by allowing it to go on accumulating. It was this same, long-term debt that stopped Matt from protesting, when, the following morning, at the very last minute, his mother decided to accompany him on the fifteen-minute walk from the house to the railway station. And so it was that they walked through the town, Matt striding ahead with the Gladstone swinging back and forth, his mother a step or two behind, smiling beatifically at all who greeted them.

'You go on back, now. I'll be fine', he said when they reached the railway station. 'And don't let Will take his nose out of his books.'

'Don't worry. He won't.' She spoke decisively, quietly pleased as she always was when Matt's concern for his brothers struck a parental note. 'Don't worry. He won't,' she said again, this time a lot less decisively, her voice fading as she looked about the station, her expression taking on an uncharacteristic blankness. Seeing Matt step into the world, equipped to make his own way forward, was a moment towards which she had worked for the greater part of her life, redoubling her efforts when her husband died. That moment had now arrived, but she was unable to embrace it, unable to seize the joy she'd imagined it would bring. It was as though the long, fretful journey had somehow sapped whatever capacity she might have had to celebrate her arrival. Or perhaps, up close, that milestone, so long a fateful marker on her horizon, now seemed insignificant.

'I'll go, so,' she said, but she didn't move.

'Yes. You go on back. I'll be fine.'

She squeezed his hand, tightening his already tight grip on the handle of the Gladstone. 'You'll be fine. I know that.'

Matt remained on the bridge watching the train wind its way across the flat landscape, soon to disappear into the first of a series of gangly outcrops, silver birches rising up from thickets of blackberry brambles and sloe bushes. As he turned around, the craning marigolds and luminous orange nasturtiums spilling out of the station window boxes caught his eye. They gave the station an old-fashioned, English look, a toy-town symmetry, boldly at odds with the sprawling landscape into which it had been plonked.

The train had made several unscheduled stops on the way, some in or near stations, others in the ripe, open countryside. It had remained for almost half an hour in one station, unidentifiable because the name had been blacked out as a security measure, while an old man and a scrawny boy wheel-barrowed turf along the platform to the engine room. Matt watched them sloping back and forward, all the while trying to envisage what it would be like to live in Rathisland, his thoughts occasionally roving back to the previous summer, 1941, to the Local Defence Force training camp at Gormanston where he'd spent the month of July. Rathisland, he figured, would be different, not least because he'd have money in his pocket.

'No use in fixing a time, the way the trains are running,' Father Finn had warned when, as instructed in the letter offering him the job, Matt had rung to arrange a meeting. Hopping from one foot to the other in the hall in his Aunt Agnes's house, Matt listened as Father Finn went on and on about the many inconveniences caused by the war, the mounting cost of the call unrelentingly pressed home by his Aunt Agnes, her face a pincushion of anxiety, hovering at the kitchen door. Phone calls, particularly long distance ones, were made only in emergencies. Aunt Agnes's phone, unlike their own, had remained in operation because her husband, Frank, was lieutenant-in-command of the town's Local Defence Force. The smell from the mouthpiece alone, that Bakelite, metallic mix with a lingering whiff of cold, human breath, was enough to trigger a sickly, low-intensity panic not just in Matt, but in any one of Aunt Agnes's friends or family courageous enough to ask to use it.

'Call in here whenever you get in,' Father Finn eventually said, officiously adding that 'suitable digs' had already been arranged.

Matt set out for the town, every now and then changing the Gladstone from one hand to the other, leaving it down for a few minutes, dallying in the cool of the overhanging hedgerows as thoughts about the future triggered a wave of excitement that carried him forward at blinding speed only to drop him in a place he didn't know, a place that filled him with apprehension.

'Matt Duggan. Father Finn is expecting me.'

He stepped forward, but the housekeeper, a dark-eyed, slow moving woman in her late forties, raised her hand like a traffic controller. 'Wait. Wait there.' When she returned she didn't speak. She just opened the inner door and, eyes and mouth downcast, pointed to the room to the right. Matt smiled, awkwardly manoeuvring his bag past her, puzzled by her expression, unaware that the 'ailing' parish priest, who Father Finn was replacing, had trained her to regard herself as a sentry, a watchdog whose duty it was to protect him from his parishioners. When someone was admitted, as they very occasionally were, she regarded it as a defeat and consequently treated them with contempt.

Father Finn stood with his back to Matt, leaning a little towards the large window, his head tilted to see beyond the towering monkey puzzle tree and the feathery pampas grass, sights fixed on the town curling complacently in on itself. Bundles of a missionary magazine were stacked tidily against the panelled wall and, in the corner, on an intricately carved plinth stood an enormous statue of Saint Joseph. Matt tried to identify the liquoricey scent, throat lozenges, he thought, something tangy at any rate, mixed with a dry, papery smell.

'A godforsaken place,' Father Finn announced solemnly before turning around.

Matt eased his bag onto the parquet floor and stepped forward with his hand outstretched. Father Finn had an all-over sheen, jet black hair, a lightweight mohair suit and shoes so highly polished that they reflected the sunlight. His eyes sparkled with what Matt initially took to be a mix of curiosity and friendliness, but turned out to be delight at the prospect of unburdening himself of the frustration he felt in being appointed, albeit temporarily, to what he variously described as the last place on earth God created, a stifling backwater, a nest of Philistines.

'Sit, please sit down,' he demanded, noisily rolling a boiled sweet from one side of his mouth to the other. He then bounced boyishly into the opposite chair.

Matt was still sitting there half an hour later, his head swimming with accounts of the many endeavours Father Finn had made during the previous winter 'to raise Rathisland out of the mire'.

'Three people turned up for the *Macbeth* auditions.' He sighed loudly, throwing his hands up in pique, anticipating an equally indignant response from Matt.

'Three people?' Matt sat upright, inflecting the words to convey an amazement he did not feel.

'Only three.' Father Finn sank back into his chair in a sulk. 'Mrs Sheridan, Miss Dunne,' he tilted his head in the direction of the door, identifying Miss Dunne as his housekeeper, 'and John Bosco.' He paused to consider whether or not he should identify John Bosco, which he then did in a dismissive sort of way, 'John Bosco Dunne, her brother.'

He sucked the sweet vigorously, pushing it to the front of his mouth and shaping his lips around it. 'Incidentally, Mrs Sheridan is … you'll meet her later, she has agreed to take you as a lodger, generously I might add because, you know …' he lowered his voice to a confidential half-whisper, '… she isn't in need of extra income. Her husband, the late Mr Sheridan, was a bank manager.'

After about an hour, Miss Dunne appeared at the door like a prison warder. She and Father Finn began to communicate in what appeared to Matt to be some sort of eyebrow code. Father Finn stood up, stretched his arms in slow motion. Then, indicating that Matt should follow, led the way to the spacious, lavender-smelling dining-room across the hall. Matt traipsed behind, trying to think of questions he might ask to show how closely he was following the animated account Father Finn was providing of the seven years he had spent in Rome prior to his arrival in Rathisland.

At first Matt didn't notice that there was only one place setting at the enormous table.

Father Finn stood directly in front of him, his hands held up and fingers splayed as if he were under arrest. When he saw that Matt was puzzled by the gesture, he began to rotate his hands, faster and faster, finally drawing them together as if to dry them with a towel. Matt copped on and began to nod. Using his head as a pointer, while continuing to dry his hands with an imaginary towel, Father Finn directed Matt out the dining-room door and up the stairs to the first landing, then down a passage to the left, at the end of which Matt would, he indicated with a solemn nod, find what he had gone to such lengths not to mention. In the cloistered modesty of that half-house, half-church, the gurgle and splash of urine felt dangerously offensive, while the torrential roar of the flushing toilet seemed altogether profane. Matt stood for a moment or two, gripping the elaborate, delicately fissured, washhand basin with both hands, looking intently in the mirror, fixing his face this way and that as he tried to settle on the expression which, in keeping with Father Finn's finicky expectations, would most effectively downplay the reason for his three-minute absence from the dining-room.

When he returned, Father Finn was holding his collar an inch or so from his neck, preparing to stuff a corner of the large, starched napkin into the space he had created.

'*Ah Bella Italia*,' he sighed, 'You'd need to see for yourself, see the fine public buildings, the roads, especially the roads, *tuto e magnifico*.' He took up his knife and fork, left them down again, almost immediately. 'I'm telling you, Benito Mussolini is a miracle worker, a genius. No question about it.'

'Yes, and the communists aren't getting much of a look in,' Matt said confidently, certain he was on safe ground with an anti-communist quip, all set to continue when Father Finn's face filled with alarm. He surveyed the room, coming to a standstill when he reached the large, rope-edged, mahogany sideboard. He glared at it suspiciously, raising his index finger to his lips as his unease deepened. It occurred to Matt that he might be trying to suggest there was someone hiding behind it, listening to their conversation, but then it became clear that this was merely a charade to impress how necessary it was to keep secret what he was about to say.

'It's felt that Mr Carmody has links.' He leaned conspiratorially towards Matt. 'Sergeant Cotton has raised the matter with me. He has links that could spell trouble.' He nodded gravely, all the while searching Matt's face for a response, overlooking, in his bid to be secretive, the possibility that Matt didn't know who Mr Carmody was. When this dawned on him he simply said, 'You'll see what I mean on Monday, when you start at the school.' Must be the headmaster, Matt thought, following Father Finn's movements as he reached for the bottle of Yorkshire Relish and splashed it energetically on the overlapping slices of marbleized, cold beef.

'Part of your duty,' he sat up authoritatively, 'a very important part, I might add, will be to inform me of anything suspicious he says or does.' With that he pronged the beef with his fork and began cutting it into long strips, curling them around his fork before adding a slice of beetroot. He lurched forward as he chewed, determined to continue speaking as soon as possible.

'The communist, you see, is capable of assuming many guises.' He paused, stared into the middle distance, creating the impression that he was speaking from memory, perhaps recalling a particular communist with whom he'd had dealings. 'So cunning, so very cunning that he may even appear as a defender, a staunch defender, of everything he secretly wishes to destroy.'

Many evenings spent discussing the evils of communism with his confrères in the Irish College in Rome had left Father Finn with an out-and-out abhorrence of communism. This did not diminish on his return home. If anything, it became more intense, finding a focus in the IRA. Though little more than a tatty remnant of the large nationalist force it had been in the period leading up to the founding of the state, the now outlawed IRA, still 'at war' with Britain, had, a few years beforehand, been infiltrated by leading figures in the small but active communist movement. It was a brief, ill-fated phase. But Father Finn, like practically all his fellow clerics, didn't see it as such and continued to regard the IRA as a front for communism.

Following the outbreak of war across Europe two years previously, a policy of neutrality was declared. In Rathisland, it fell to Garda Sergeant Cotton to identify anyone likely to jeopardize that policy. This, in effect, meant identifying IRA supporters, those who might pave the way for a German take-over in order to bring about the defeat of Britain. IRA men from all over the country had been rounded up and interned, while those whose links with the organization were seen as too tenuous to pose a serious threat were, thereon in, closely monitored. Consequently, Sergeant Cotton, shortly after Father Finn's arrival in Rathisland, called late one afternoon to alert him to Mr Carmody's known, but supposedly past connections with the IRA. And Father Finn, in keeping with his firmly anchored idea of what the IRA were actually about, straight away fixed on the notion that he was a communist.

What came into Matt's mind when Father Finn confided this concern to him were atrocities from the Spanish Civil War attributed to communists: nuns roasting to death in burning convents, dead children strewn on the streets of eerily empty towns; scenes that had appeared in the pages of the *Catholic Enquirer* and had been posted on the notice board in the main hall of his secondary school, St Augustine's.

'Is there something, something in particular I should be on the lookout for?' he asked, keen to meet Father Finn's expectations, but at the same time inclined to dismiss his concern as scaremongering.

The doorknocker sounded; a loud, resounding thud, followed by a succession of quick, short raps. Father Finn scowled at his heavily laden fork.

'Everything. You will need to note everything.' He tucked his napkin further down behind his collar. 'What seems insignificant to you, may appear altogether different to the trained eye.' Tilting his knife towards his face he moved it up and down mechanically in front of his right eye.

The voices at the front door grew louder. He strained to listen.

The dining-room door opened. Just a little, no more than a few inches. Miss Dunne slipped in like a fish passing through a closed hand, tugging the shoulders of her crossover apron forward before she spoke:

'Josie and Kathleen Bergin, Mrs Byrne's sisters, are outside, saying one of the Byrnes is dying. Agnes. The youngest one. The doctor is just after leaving. Said there was no use in him coming back.'

Father Finn weighed up the information, then removed and folded his napkin. He beckoned Miss Dunne to come closer.

'The Byrnes?' he half-whispered, extending the word, obliquely asking Miss Dunne if they were the sort of family who went in for hysteria, if, in short, it could be a false alarm. Visibly fearful of the authority vested in her, Miss Dunne shook her head violently. He sprung up, replaced his chair with military precision, instructed Miss Dunne to direct Matt to Mrs Sheridan's house on the Square, shook hands and left.

The relief Matt felt, like a cool breeze on a torpidly hot day, made him shudder.

'It's on the Square, between the two banks,' Miss Dunne snapped, then stood staring at him. 'Your bag is out in the porch.'

A great, sprawling cedar darkened the entire front of the house, stretching so close along one section that it formed a tunnel in which the resinous, clove-like scent of the tree was mildly intoxicating. Matt inhaled sharply, holding that scent while following the trail it created to Christmas at home in Ballbriggan. Sixteen weeks, he thought, raising the Gladstone. Sixteen weeks. He put his hand in his pocket, closing it slowly around the piece of light, crumpled cardboard, the luggage label he'd pulled off his bag and stuffed into his pocket as soon as his mother left the station. His grip on it loosened as he recalled how tightly she tied it on, knot after knot after knot.

Chapter 2

Matt knocked on Mrs Sheridan's front door and stood back a little while he tried to decide how he ought to introduce himself. He could hear movement inside, light footsteps, then a door closing. He drew breath, certain someone was approaching. When nobody arrived he began to wonder if he should knock again. After a moment or two, he reached for the highly polished knocker, raising it a little, on the point of striking it down when the door began to open. Standing there, with her head slightly tilted to one side, was a woman in her early sixties, her greying hair brushed back to form a smooth, shallow cone at either side. Her necklace, a single string of large pearls, sparkled with a myriad of yellowish flecks cast by the mustard coloured cardigan and jumper she was wearing

'You must be Mr Duggan.' She extended her hand and smiled as she said, 'How do you do?'

'Yes. Well thanks. Matt. Matt Duggan.' He leaned forward to shake her hand, catching the vaguely chemical scent of her cologne.

'Please. Come in.' She stood back, creating a narrow space through which Matt passed, conscious, as he always was in restricted spaces, of his height. Mrs Sheridan angled her head to take stock of his size as though estimating how much he would eat.

'You didn't have any difficulty finding ...'

'No,' Matt cut in, 'it's great to have digs within walking distance of the school.'

Mrs Sheridan's eyelids flickered, closing lightly as she strained to find a way of telling him she didn't like to think of her house as a digs.

'Father Finn, you see ...' Her face softened, urging him to anticipate what she was about to say, to acknowledge that he knew Father Finn was behind her decision to take a lodger.

Matt nodded, but much as he felt he ought to, he couldn't bring himself to speak. Another encounter like the one he'd just had with Father Finn, another round of coded *politesse*, was more than he could bear. Besides, he figured he was already in possession of enough pieces of the jigsaw to form the whole picture; Father Finn, aware of how empty Mrs Sheridan's life had become since her husband's death, had prevailed on her to take a lodger in the belief that it would give a focus to her days.

She showed him around the downstairs part of the house; the kitchen, the scullery, the dining-room, relying mainly on gestures and pauses, intent on appearing inexperienced, behaving in the opposite way to how she imagined a hardened landlady might. She stood facing the closed door of the drawing-room, her papery, freckled hand folded around the delft knob. When she opened it, she didn't go directly in. She just stood in the fiery bolt of late August sunlight that was blazing through the window, affectionately surveying the room. Eventually, she stepped inside, indicating to Matt that he should follow. He positioned himself beside her, an uncomfortable witness to her wistful gazing. She went over to the piano, a baby grand that took up most of the room. She stood there expectantly, hands clasped, bracing herself as if she might at any moment burst into song. Matt saw the opportunity to strike up a conversation, to ask a question about the piano, unleash those memories that the instrument, almost human in its presence, seemed to be evoking. But he couldn't summon the enthusiasm to ask that, or indeed any other, question. He felt overwhelmed by the formality, the taut intensity, of it all. He longed for the easy, jocular intimacy he shared with his brothers and inadvertently began to plan how he would portray Father Finn and Mrs Sheridan to them.

'The stairs.' Mrs Sheridan pointed down the hall from the drawing-room door. 'Yours is the first room. On the right. ' Her hand coiled upwards. The rank scent of the geranium, spindling out of a free-standing cachepot beside the front door, gave way to a whiff of Brasso, which Matt traced to the gleaming stair-rods. He could not wait to be on his own, to drift away freely with those warm thoughts of home now filling his head, to feel the ease of slumping into the green sofa in the kitchen. And all the while, the account of the afternoon he was piecing together for his brothers was gathering pace, and competing with, soon to eclipse completely, the directions Mrs Sheridan was giving to the bathroom.

The stairs, she said, pointing to the stairs as though I didn't know what a fucking stairs looked like. He heard his brothers laugh, inadvertently smiled, prompting Mrs Sheridan to smile nervously. In a bid to banish them from his thoughts, he glanced around for something he might comment on, quick to point at a tennis racket wedged in between an umbrella and a polished blackthorn stick on the hall stand.

'Do you play?' Mrs Sheridan asked as he searched for something to say about it.

'Yes,' he said, grasping the opportunity, hardly registering that it was a lie.

'Oh good.' She pursed her lips, tilted her head and looked squarely up at him for the first time. 'Then maybe you'd consider playing on Saturday? Against Abbeyleix. So few men now. Scarcely enough for a doubles ladder.'

Her eyes tightened, willing him to agree.

'Alright,' he said, gripping the banister, one foot already firmly planted on the first step.

'Oh, good.' She beamed. 'It'll make such a difference.'

Matt held the Gladstone in front of him, manoeuvring it up the stairs like a Roman shield.

'Such a difference,' she repeated, infusing the words with relief as though he had volunteered to strike a blow for some great cause. 'Supper will be at six forty-five …'

'That's grand,' he called from the landing, adding 'thanks' after a second or two, vaguely resentful at hearing his voice fill a house that he did not wish to regard as home.

Mrs Sheridan made her way to the kitchen, using the fingers of her right, then her left hand, to draw up a list of the foodstuffs she had in the house, lamenting as she frequently did, the difficulties caused by rationing.

Matt closed his bedroom door behind him, his head ringing with the clamour of a self on hold all afternoon.

'Christ,' he blurted out as he sat on the bed, ruffling the hospital-taut counterpane.

He stood up, careful to remain stooped until he was no longer in danger of banging his head on the sloping ceiling. Over by the window, holding the thick, lace curtain to one side he looked out on the Square, as a thin, gangly girl, standing close to the metal pump in the middle, hoisted an overflowing bucket up and off the spout.

'Ladies and Gentlemen, may I present to you a man whose genius …' His brother Hugh's words, echoing in his ears, his mother feigning exasperation in the background. He allowed the curtain to fall back into place, took the crumpled luggage label out of his pocket, placed it on the chest of drawers and began to smooth it out.

Mr Matt Duggan NT. He swallowed hard, determined to resist those thoughts which, if given a chance, would trigger feelings he considered babyish. He opened the Gladstone and began to search for the packet of cream stationery his mother had slipped down the side just before he left for the train.

Dear Hugh and Will, he began, *I don't know what sort of a place I've come to. When I arrived at the parish priest's house a half-woman, half-dragon answered the door* … and on he went, smiling to himself, imagining Hugh and Will smiling, so absorbed in describing it all that the rest of the afternoon slipped by unnoticed. Around six, with suppertime on the horizon, he began to loose concentration and decided to finish the letter after supper.

The first thing that struck Matt, as he entered the small, dark dining-room, was the quantity of cutlery lined up on either side of the place mat. The table at home in Balbriggan was a knife-and-fork table, except for Sunday when a dessert spoon was added. He examined the marble-sized, ridged balls of butter, all stacked to form a pyramid on a china plate, so meticulously sculpted that they seemed more like ornaments than food. The smell of frying pudding, seeping in from the kitchen, hung about the room like an intoxicating vapour, edging the hunger he felt to the brink of delirium. In a single swooping movement he snatched a slice of brown bread from the semicircle of slices fanning out from the cut loaf, pushed it into his mouth, swallowing it almost whole just as the piercing pips signalling the six-forty-five news sounded. The tense bristle of expectation raised by those pips, however, quickly gave way to monotony as sparse wisps of war news trickled from the radio. There was a report about North Africa where a battle of biblical proportions had been raging, delivered with such remoteness on that August evening that it might well have been a chess match. Unlike Balbriggan, it wasn't possible to get the BBC in Rathisland, at least not clearly, so Radio Éireann, rigidly censored to uphold the state's policy of neutrality, was the only source of war news.

He spotted an open copy of *Dublin Opinion* in the magazine rack beside the fireplace and was about to pick it up when Mrs Sheridan's head and arm appeared through the narrowly opened door leading to the kitchen.

'Ready in a jiff. Sit, sit down. You might like to look at this while you're waiting.' She handed him a small manila envelope then slid back into the kitchen.

Hardly a bill, Matt thought, very peculiar if it is, a possibility he then dismissed, but still began to prepare an explanation as to why he couldn't pay it, not until the end of the month at any rate. The writing was minuscule, so small in places that it was initially illegible. He saw the word *socks*, then thought it must be something to do with laundry arrangements. Bit by bit he deciphered the words.

Discist from what you're doing or you'll get your own parcel and there won't be socks or barnbracks in it.

One thing for sure, it wasn't intended for him. That much was clear. He wondered if Mrs Sheridan knew what it was about. Was she asking him to interpret what it meant? Either way, he suspected it was in some way sinister and so began to search for an angle from which to condemn it. He continued to try and make sense of it, but made no headway. He then honed in on the mistakes, ready when Mrs Sheridan came in, to point out that *desist* was incorrectly spelt, and furthermore that *barnbrack* was a misuse, the correct word, coming from the Irish for speckled cake, being barmbrack. But he didn't get the opportunity to alert her to these mistakes. Holding a steaming plate in one hand and teapot in the other, she was already speaking when she came into the room.

'Of course I brought it straight to the barracks, straight to Sergeant Cotton.'

'Of course,' Matt repeated mechanically, all the while monitoring the descent of the plate, the size and variety of the grill making him feel uneasy at first, then guilty about the way in which he had portrayed her to his brothers.

'He said there was nothing to worry about, that he knew who it was. Well, not for certain, but that it was just mischief. She nodded in the direction of the plate she was holding with oven gloves. 'Anyway, in the end he sent it to Dublin to have it examined by a detective.'

'Who? Who was it?' Matt spoke forcibly, giving the impression that he had definite views on how the matter ought to have been handled.

'The name Costigan was mentioned, but it meant nothing to me.' Mrs Sheridan stood back a little once she had safely eased down the overflowing plate, then leaned forward again to cover the teapot with a bulky, hand knitted cosy. 'It may need to draw for a bit. It was really just a misunderstanding. Something I happened to suggest at an ICA meeting.'

Wide-eyed at the sight of so much food, Matt did not respond.

'The Irish Country Women's Association,' she explained, thinking Matt did not know what the ICA was.

'Yes. The Irish Country Women's Association.' He spoke without looking up from his plate.

With a flurry of fast finger movements, a short, silent piano scale, Mrs Sheridan indicated that he should begin eating, which he already had. He put his knife and fork down, drew his chair a little closer to the table, then began again. Mrs Sheridan winced as she watched him draw the chair in without taking his weight off it, sure from the cracking sound that he had damaged the spine. She smiled in an effort to conceal her concern, drawing breath tersely as she prepared to speak.

'What the sergeant said was that whoever wrote it wasn't there – at the meeting. They just heard about it. And that it was a man.'

'How? I mean how did he figure out it was a man?'

She drew her chin tightly into her neck. 'Barmbracks to the Front? Who ever heard the like? I mean even if that much fruit could be got. '

'True.'

'Such a cowardly thing, an anonymous letter.' Her gaze settled on the row of silver-framed photographs on the mantelpiece.

Matt's mouth was too full to reply.

'My mother was part of it. In the Great War. Everyone was.' She spoke wistfully, holding her gaze on the photographs. 'The place looked like a drapery shop when I arrived home that Christmas. Socks and scarves in piles all over the drawing-room, ready for wrapping.' She stirred the air with her hand as if to point these things out. 'Both my uncles, my mother's brothers, you see, had volunteered. As soon as the war broke out, nineteen ...' She made the word hum, extending it like a musical note, '... nineteen whatever it was.'

'Fourteen.'

'Yes. Long before all that other business started.'

Matt looked up from his plate, expecting her to elaborate, explain what she meant *by all that other business*. When she didn't he reckoned she meant the 1916 Rebellion and the War of Independence, slowing the pace at which he was chewing, more than a little taken aback to hear those fateful events described in so offhand a way.

'I really only suggested *parcels for the Front* to get the idea of helping across. It could have been, I mean I might just as easily have said medicine. Bandages and whatnot for the Red Cross.' Mrs Sheridan shrugged her shoulders as if to rein in her indignation.

Matt figured she must have proposed to the ICA that they start a parcels-for-the-troops scheme in Rathisland. But she must, he surmised, have taken the proposal a step further, possibly challenged those who were opposed to it, because just proposing it alone could hardly have provoked an anonymous threat. There were lots of similar locally organized schemes in operation. Matt's next-door neighbours in Balbriggan, the Dolans, were involved in one launched earlier that year by the doctor's wife, Mrs Spellman. She had got families in the locality who kept poultry to breed bantams, because their eggs, with tougher shells than those of other chickens, were more likely to survive the journey to the various military bases in Britain to which they were sent, supposedly for dispatch to the Front.

'Quite a few at the meeting thought it was a good idea. They told me so afterwards.' She threw her head back defiantly.

'If I was out there, out on any of the Fronts, I'd be glad to get a parcel.' Words that grew limp even as Matt uttered them, unable, as he was, to envisage the 'out there' to which he'd referred, let alone imagine himself getting a parcel. Even the word *war* itself had undergone a change of meaning. It

27

conjured places with far-fetched names, an otherness about them that flared brightly for a few seconds then whittled away into the darkness. The word had been commandeered to denote shortages of one sort or another, neutered to such an extent that it no longer evoked carnage. In and around Rathisland it was almost always referred to as *the duration*, not its official name, *the Emergency*. Mrs Sheridan made a point of using neither of these terms. To her it was always *the war*. Her war, everyone's war.

'I wouldn't pay any attention to it. It's just some crank with nothing better to do.' Matt reached for the teapot, withdrawing as Mrs Sheridan's hand swooped in.

'Mind you, only Mrs Thompson and her sister-in-law voted for it.' When she left the teapot down she picked up the envelope from beside Matt's plate, took out the letter, scrutinized it as though there was some detail or other still to be unearthed, something hidden in among the words that might make it less threatening. She then folded it, put it back into the manila envelope and slipped it into the pocket of her house coat, all the while watching Matt drag a crust across the plate, mopping up every last drop of the egg-laced juices and pudding-speckled oils. It was a gesture of appreciation, an accolade he assumed she would happily accept. But her eyes, as though blinded by a sudden burst of light, clamped shut and her head spun abruptly to one side. He manoeuvred the soggy crust towards his mouth, expecting to eat it unobserved when her head spun back again, her face brimming with purpose.

'I'm glad to have a ...' she hesitated, 'someone under the roof at night. Not that I mind being alone.' She rushed to pick up the plate and brought it directly into the kitchen.

When she returned she was no longer wearing a housecoat. Her loose, floral dress waved a little as she walked, making her seem less elderly. She'd decided that she'd acquitted herself satisfactorily as a landlady, and could now relax. Matt listened as she outlined her day-to-day routine, her voice pitched to create a busyness about her many commitments. As secretary of Rathisland Lawn Tennis Club, on its last legs when she joined its complacent committee, she had spent much of the summer organizing the restoration of the two courts. As well as that, she gave a weekly class in the technical school on what she fussily dismissed as 'making do'. These classes set out to demonstrate ways of minimizing the impact of food rationing. They included instruction on how to prepare alternatives to staples such as tea, which she often concocted in advance. Various berries and weeds, dandelion and the like, had to be gathered and sorted, giving the kitchen the look of an apothecary's laboratory, sometimes filling the whole house with a urine-like stench. Some weeks previously, she'd been appointed social secretary of the golf club, which often required her to work late into the night, sorting score cards, filling in competition tables, ticking off names on the Silver Circle list. So taking a lodger was not, as Matt had assumed earlier, a way of filling her days. It was a bid for company. A way of ensuring there was someone else in the house, particularly at night. And, as Matt would happily learn, an attempt to resume a routine she'd had for over twenty years of marriage to Benny; a routine in which a hearty supper on a promisingly set table at six forty-five was pivotal.

He picked up, in a piecemeal way, that the previous year, when her husband Benny had retired as manager of the Munster & Leinster Bank in Fermoy they had come to live in Rathisland. He had been an assistant manager in the town for most of the twenties and during those years they were part of what Mrs Sheridan nostalgically called 'a crowd'. The impression Matt formed was of a group whose weekends were taken up with golf and tennis in the summer, and in the winter, card games and 'the occasional sherry do'. When Mr Sheridan was posted elsewhere they were sorry to leave and decided, not straight away, but a few years later, to buy a house in the town, intending to spend their retirement there.

'Benny was in the best of health,' she told Matt several times, each time looking vacantly around the room, infusing the silence with the same mix of lament and forbearance, a stance she took out of conviction, a quiet form of heroism, a way of telling Matt that she was determined not to complain, even though she had plenty to complain about.

Back in his room that evening Matt began to reread the letter he'd been writing to Hugh and Will, growing more and more uncomfortable with his comic descriptions of Mrs Sheridan. Before he'd finished reading the second page, where he'd drawn a comparison between her and their Aunt Agnes, he crumpled the letter up, sat down, and started again.

Chapter 3

A mix of chimney soot and acrid drain fumes formed a permanent background to a variety of seasonal smells in the school building; clothes with a wet-dog whiff, rancid canvas shoes, molten, turf tar. But the overwhelming odour in Mr Carmody's classroom, to which Matt went directly on arrival at the school on Monday morning, was tobacco smoke. The newly lit, moist-ended cigarette hanging from his lower lip bobbed up and down as he spoke.

'All I can say is I hope you're here longer than the last fellow. Went off to get himself killed by the Germans.' He twisted his index finger forcibly into his temple.

Matt did not consider for a moment reporting anything Carmody said, or did, to Father Finn, even if he did turn out to be a communist. But while he considered this highly unlikely the notion had somehow taken root, prompting him to look beyond the literal meaning of almost everything Carmody said, searching, despite himself, for evidence of communistic beliefs. This slowed up his responses, made him seem hesitant and measured.

'At least they didn't send a dwarf,' Carmody said, sizing him up and down. Matt grew increasingly self-conscious, misgivings about the elaborate lesson plans he'd prepared mounting as piercing shrieks, underscored by a persistent hum, filtered through the closed door leading onto the corridor where the pupils were jostling for places in the class lines.

'Any trouble, send them straight to me.' Carmody pointed to himself authoritatively. 'No harm in a few dead crows.'

Matt stared at him blankly.

'Dead crows, y'know, to frighten the live ones.' He guffawed but at the same time his eyes narrowed, scrutinizing Matt suspiciously; was he stupid, or just pretending to be stupid?

'Dead crows!' Matt laughed, relieved when Carmody, who continued to scrutinize him, clasped his hands together like an MC heralding the next act in a performance. Matt braced himself, hoping for an opportunity to make an impression, but Carmody just turned around and headed for the rickety cupboard at the other side of the room. And he remained there, staring into the cupboard for what seemed like an eternity, the fug of cigarette smoke around his head growing more and more dense. The pitch of voices coming from the corridor escalated. Carmody took three oblong Department of Education roll books out and, clenching two under his arm, held the third out. Matt rushed over.

'I better get going. Face the music.' Matt smiled, now more conscious than ever of his failure to make a good impression.

The walls of the poorly ventilated room in which he took fourth and fifth class were chalky grey, splotched with brownish jagged circles where a layer of the distemper had flaked off. The lower sections were dotted with thousands of tiny pale-blue blobs, testimony to the age-old ink war between the two classes. The floor, worn to chaff in the aisles between the desks, was pocked with dark bumps created by knots and gnarls in the timber.

All forty-six pupils followed his every move as he put his case on the desk, sat down, took his pen out of his lapel pocket, unscrewed the top, opened the roll book and fixed his attention on the long list of names. Any mishap, however minor would, he knew, trigger a reaction from the silently staring pupils, so he proceeded with extreme care, intent on avoiding direct eye contact until he was fully ready to call the roll.

'Albert Behan.'

There was an immediate outburst of laughter. Matt stood up, his whole face tightening to form the sternest expression he could muster.

'Albert Behan. Is Albert Behan here?' A fresh outburst of laughter that rapidly turned into a mocking, hee-haw chant as Matt looked about the room searching for someone he could hold responsible for what was happening.

'Bain,' someone called out. 'Put your hand up, y'eejit.'

Using one arm to lever the other upwards, a large-faced boy, blushing so intensely that his outsize ears, visibly throbbing, identified himself to Matt.

'Bertie Bain. Sir.'

Matt looked at him, trying to figure out what he ought to do next.

'Bertie Bain. Sir. Me name is Bertie Bain.'

'Behan. Albert Behan.' Matt spoke emphatically, determined to get on with the roll call.

'Yes Sir. Bain. Bertie Bain.'

More laughter.

'Quiet,' Matt demanded loudly, both taken aback and

relieved at the silence that followed. He sat down, scanned the list of names, quickly noting those that might trigger another outbreak. Nothing he'd learned in the training school had prepared him for the battle of wits in which he now found himself. Directing questions to the class in general, he proceeded with the roll call, which degenerated into a free-for-all, a cacophony of finger clicking, roars of, 'Sir, Sir … *A Mháistir, A Mháistir*', several of the raised hands swooping to wallop whoever happened to be sitting in the desk in front, loud laughter if he directed a question to a weak student, someone the others knew to be incapable of answering correctly.

The air in the classroom, clammy from the outset, was soon almost unbreathable. Stealing a glance at the fogged-up windows, he tried to figure out how the pulley cords to open them worked. Most were densely tangled and bunched into knots at the tops of the windows, well out of reach. Getting at them would mean climbing up on the sills, four feet or thereabouts from the ground. Better leave it until break, he decided, but the air became so stifling that he had no choice but to investigate. The humming behind him as he examined the nearest window fizzled to silence, then to some ominous point beyond as he reached for a pulley cord that appeared to be within his grasp. Stretching as far up as possible he managed, with a short leap, to grab it. He tried to uncoil it, but made no headway. If anything, it became more tangled. He tugged it towards him. Nothing happened.

'That one's broke sir.' A high-pitched voice pierced the silence.

'How do they work anyway?' Matt asked.

Three, four, five boys leapt to their feet instantly, jostling each other out of the way as they scrambled up onto the windowsill. Once up they held their position by stamping their hobnailed boots on the fingers of anyone who tried to join them. Within seconds the classroom was like a rodeo, with pupils leaping bronco-style around the place, while a skinny boy with matchstick legs shimmied up the side of the window, intent on releasing the jammed pulley cord.

'Come down. Come down out of there immediately,' Matt roared in alarm: all heads swivelled in his direction, many of them about to swivel back to watch the progress of the monkey boy, when Matt warned that whoever wasn't back, sitting quietly at their desk within a minute, would be sent straight out to Mr Carmody. He couldn't believe the impact Carmody's name had. Almost before he could draw breath to repeat what he'd said, every last pupil was back at his desk. Not a sound, not a movement, so eerily quiet that for the remaining half-hour or so before break he stayed on high alert, all the time expecting another outburst. As soon as the last row of pupils had left the classroom for the school yard Matt climbed up onto the nearest window sill, untangled the coiled pulley cords and drew them down, inhaling deeply as the first wave of cool, clean air swept into the classroom.

'Aren't you coming?'

He swung around, pleased to hear an adult voice, quick to realize that the man standing in the doorway was the first- and second-class teacher.

'We go down to Mr Carmody's room for the breaks. I'm next door. Brendan. Brendan Canning.'

Matt leapt down from the sill.

Brendan Canning, who was in his early thirties, had been teaching in the school for nine years. He had, Matt noted as he approached to shake hands, a peculiar appearance, a small, bony head with sandy hair cropped so tightly that he could easily have been mistaken for the inmate of an institution, a prison or a psychiatric hospital. Following him down the corridor to Carmody's room Matt couldn't avoid staring at his shoes, shoes that were so large and expansive at the toes that each time they hit the ground they flapped like those of a circus clown.

'Well. How are you finding it?' he asked Matt as they entered Carmody's room.

'It's fine. Grand.' Matt spoke hesitantly, unsure if Canning had heard the commotion caused by his attempt to open the windows, inclined to think that he had when Canning said, 'Anytime they're restless the best thing is to get them *ag canadh*. Singing,' he added, addressing Matt in the same way as he addressed his pupils, habitually using an Irish word or phrase, which he then translated.

'Singing,' Carmody sneered, then looked directly at Matt.

'Did you bring a stick with you? Because if you didn't, my advice to you is to take one from here before you do another thing.' And, crooking his index finger several times in quick succession he indicated to Matt to follow as he led the way over to the rickety cupboard. Flinging open both doors he pointed to the lowest shelf on which five different sticks were laid out like artefacts in a museum.

'The choice isn't as big as you think. That one gives splinters if you use the thin end. And this one,' Carmody reached for a carved chair leg, 'is for special occasions.' He smiled ruefully at Matt. 'So the choice is down to these two. The bamboo or the sally. It's up to yourself.'

Matt looked over at Canning who was nodding decisively, urging him to choose.

'The bamboo. I'll take the bamboo,' Matt blurted, reaching into the cupboard as he might reach into a dark, unsafe space, a badger sett or a stoat burrow in which his hand might suddenly be bitten.

He didn't plan to use the bamboo but nonetheless placed it in a prominent place on his desk after break, uneasy and at the same time reassured by the reaction it provoked in the pupils as they traipsed back into the classroom. Canning's advice to get them singing, however, was much more useful. That afternoon, with the windows flung open. Matt led the pupils through the first verse of the national anthem, delighted by the enthusiasm with which they threw themselves into learning it.

'You were right about the singing,' he said as he caught up with Canning on the way out of the school gate.

'Doesn't always work, but you get to know when it will and when it won't.' Canning nodded as he spoke, then drew his lips resolutely together as though to affirm what he'd just said. Pleased that Matt had taken his advice, he set about giving more. He conjured up one situation after another in which Matt could find his authority undermined, then following through with a detailed menu of strategies he could use to reassert that authority. Every few seconds, his tightly cropped bullet head swivelled in Matt's direction to check if he was taking the lesson on board.

'The smart alec is the one to watch out for, the boyo with the grin who gets others to do his mischief for him. The best thing is to start the day by firing questions at him, questions he can't answer, take the grin off his puss.'

Intrigued, but at same time overwhelmed by all that Canning was telling him, Matt began to look out for an opportunity to steer the conversation in a different direction. That opportunity arrived when about halfway down Main Street Canning came to the end of a list of circumstances under which pupils should be sent out to Carmody.

'It's hard to make him out. Mr Carmody, I mean.'

Canning didn't reply, prompting Matt to add, as speculatively as he could, 'I mean, it's hard to get the measure of him.'

'You'll get the measure of him alright.' He laughed.

'Father Finn said he had communist links?'

'Mr Carmody is a well-respected man. Besides it's not up to you or me to be sitting in judgment on him.'

'No. I'm just saying what Father Finn said.'

'Well, that isn't up to us. That's best left to the Almighty.' Canning pursed his lips and nodded decisively.

'Best left to the Almighty …' Matt thought, thrown by the speed with which Canning had turned the tables, making him feel presumptuous and judgmental; feelings that acted like a call to arms to his brothers Hugh and Will.

'Sanctimonious bollocks.' Hugh's voice was so clear that Matt almost looked around, wishing in the same instant he could be home.

Visits from Carmody were frequent and unpredict-able. On Thursday afternoon of that first week he burst in, eyes beaming like searchlights under scowling eyebrows, an urgency about him that led Matt to think he'd come looking for someone in particular, a pupil who had committed some serious offence. All heads, as if by mechanical action, bowed. All eyelids flicked down simultaneously. He stood there, waiting, it seemed, for one of them to look up, creating an imaginary arc as he brought the cane, clutched in his right hand, to rest in slow, calculated motion on his outstretched left hand. Fear, like a poisonous gas, rose up from the mute class. He indicated that Matt should continue with the lesson.

Flustered by his presence, Matt tore through the poetry book, *Dánta na hÉireann*, looking for the poem he'd been reading aloud. Unable to find it, he rushed back to the index, then scrambled to the page and took up where he'd left off;

> Tá Tír na nÓg ar chúl an tí,
> Tír álainn trína chéile,

Locht ceithre cos ag súil gach slí,
Gan bróga orthu ná léine,
Gan Béarla acu ná Gaeilge.

The pace at which he was reading grew faster and faster. Words collided and merged clumsily into each other as he galloped towards the last line. Once there, he looked up, relieved that the reading was over but at the same time apprehensive. Carmody's cane was now swinging loosely by his side. His fierce, interrogating glare had turned to a curious smile. When he spoke his voice sounded altogether different. Neither jocular nor insinuating, it was charged with disbelief:

'Tell me.' His nose crinkled into a questioning grimace. 'How did a city lad like you get so fluent?'

Matt searched his face for irony. He knew how badly he'd read the poem, rushing through it with little or no regard for its lilting, sing-song rhythm. He knew his command of Irish was far from perfect. Despite being awarded a class prize for the subject in his final year at secondary school, he'd found himself struggling to keep up during his two years in the teacher training college where total fluency was taken for granted. There were several native speakers in his year, fellows from Kerry and Galway, who regularly spoke Irish among themselves.

Matt, irked that he'd been called a city lad, tried to think of an unchallenging way of reminding Carmody that he'd grown up in County Dublin, Balbriggan, not the city. Carmody had in fact made much of that distinction when, the previous day, he'd summoned Matt to his room to complete some Department of Education forms.

'Balbriggan ...' Matt said hesitantly, adding, as incidentally as he could, 'Not the city.'

Carmody shook his head in amazement.

'Well wherever you got it, it's the finest Irish I've heard since I came to this school. And that's neither today nor yesterday. Here, recite it again.' He flung his hand carelessly in the direction of the cowed class. 'Go on, read it. It'll do them the power of good to hear their native tongue spoken like it should be.' He nodded enthusiastically at the poetry book.

It struck Matt that the standard had been so high in his year group in the training college that he'd come to underestimate his fluency. He recalled the prize he'd been given in secondary school, an inscribed hardback copy of *Leabhar Sheáin Í Chonaill* by Séamus O Duilearga, and buoyed up by that memory as well as Carmody's flattery, he drew a deep breath, determined to put everything he had into the recital:

> *Tá Tír na nÓg ar chúl an tí,*
> *Tír álainn trína chéile,*
> *Locht ceithre cos ag súil gach slí,*
> *Gan bróga orthu ná léine,*
> *Gan Béarla acu na Gaeilge.*

'By God.' Carmody's awe was palpable. 'Step over here a minute.'

Matt followed him as he made his way towards the open door.

'Look. There's a bit of translating someone wants done. From the wireless. You'd be a topper. What d'you say?' He stood in the doorway, his back to the class.

'I don't think I'd be …'

'Are you joking me?' he said loudly, prompting some of the pupils to glance furtively in their direction.

'Translating from the wireless? I mean, is it a match or what?'

Suddenly, as though there had been an explosion in the classroom, Carmody swung around and, hunched like a prowling leopard, paced up and down in front of the motionless class.

'Well?' he demanded, straightening up as he returned to the doorway.

'If you think I'd be ...'

'No bother to you.'

Matt's reluctance receded as he fixed on the idea that the radio broadcast Carmody was asking him to translate was a match commentary. They were frequently in Irish. He'd never had much difficulty following them.

'Alright. I'll give it a go. When is it? What match is it?'

Carmody tilted his head to one side, looked up blankly at Matt as though distracted by some stray thought or other.

'To be honest, to be honest, I don't know whether it's a match or not. It's for a fellow by the name of Coll. Out on the Castle Wall Road. Dixie Coll. Tomorrow evening, sometime around seven.' He stared down at the floor, concentrating as if to calculate the space between their shoes.

'Tomorrow evening?'

Carmody drew breath as though he was about to say something, but just nodded decisively.

Matt tried to figure out how there could be a match commentary on the radio at seven on a Friday. Must be a replay, he thought, his attention diverted to the directions Carmody, using his cane as a pointer, was giving to Dixie Coll's house.

'I'd have done it myself, done it no trouble ...' Carmody said emphatically, lowering his voice and leaning a little towards Matt, '... but you see the wife's sister is coming in on the seven o'clock and I have to be at the station.' He raised his eyes, indicating he had no choice in the matter.

Something of Carmody's presence lingered in the classroom for the remainder of the afternoon, a presence Matt reluctantly welcomed because of the quiet it brought. When the school day ended he set about preparing for the following day, checking the inkwells, unrolling and flattening chart sheets, taking down the map he'd been using to teach the counties of Ireland, all the while working his way piecemeal through a simultaneous translation of a hurling match commentary.

Chapter 4

Mrs Sheridan moved the Irish-English dictionary Matt brought down to supper several times as she made space for this and that on the table, each time dallying a little, giving him an opportunity to tell her where he was bringing it. Unaware of her interest, he didn't refer to it until he stood up to leave.

'I'm in a bit of a rush. Mr Carmody asked me to do some translating.' He tapped the dictionary with his finger. 'I've to be there at seven.'

'Oh you'll be in plenty of time.' She smiled, assuming he was meeting Carmody in the school.

Matt glanced at the ormolu clock on the mantelpiece, about to explain that the translation was for someone who lived two miles outside the town, when he saw it was already quarter to seven.

He had misgivings about bringing the dictionary from the outset. He knew there wouldn't be time to use it while he was actually translating the broadcast, but figured it could be useful afterwards if he wanted to check on something he'd been doubtful about. Besides, he felt it would make him look the part. And so it did, there, striding out the Castle Wall Road, an official tome clasped under his arm, its bottle-green spine and gold embossed lettering conveying an image of expertise which, in between bolts of doubt about his ability to translate the broadcast, he enjoyed.

Seedy foxgloves and long, blackberry-laden brambles lurched out from the hedgerows lining the lane down to Colls' yard. He kept to the grassy ridge in the centre, sights set on the loose cluster of ramshackle outbuildings ahead. The stir of cattle at the other side of the hedge broke into a gallop, a loose, pounding sound softening to a low thud as they crossed the field. The lingering pelt whiff, whisked up by fleets of roused dung flies, filtered, intermittently, through the hedgerow. A hoarse, relentless dog bark came from the nearest outbuilding. All at once he wished he hadn't brought the dictionary; there was something stuffy about walking into the yard with it, something about the easy disarray of the place that made it seem peculiar. He began to look for a place to hide it, somewhere it might not get damaged, but everywhere along that last stretch of the lane seemed to carry some sort of risk. Too difficult to get at. Damp. Too visible. Soon he was in the yard, heading over to the house, too late to do anything with it.

'Hello. Hello, there.' The voice came from the open door of the largest of the outbuildings as he walked past.

'Here. In here.'

He stooped to avoid banging his head on the lintel. 'Mr Carmody asked me …' he began, straightening up before he continued with the remainder of what he'd been planning to say when he arrived.

'Shush …' Hissed a man sitting at a makeshift workbench,

his head tilted towards the innards of a wireless, his left hand extended in Matt's direction.

The light cast by the open door into the windowless outhouse illuminated the space around the entrance, weakening as it penetrated beyond, failing altogether to reach the corners. He made his way over, hand extended, adjusting to the darkness as he went, taking care not to trip over the assortment of mechanical bric-a-brac, drums of sump oil, stacks of corroding car batteries.

The hand was filthy, the elephant-grey skin a matrix of oil-clogged fissures. Matt shook it, but it remained extended, the fingers now pointing limply to the space to his right.

'It's Dixie Coll. Isn't it?'

The man nodded, his ear pressed as close to the wireless as possible, his thumb and index finger delicately edging the tuning knob forward, a millimetre at a time.

'It was as clear as a bell last night. Clear …'. Suddenly, his face lit up. A song, 'Come back to Érin', sailed confidently into range. He grinned at Matt, but almost immediately the voice began to fade. His face twitched with concern. He turned the tuning knob a fraction, scratched his head urgently. Bit by bit he coaxed the singer into range again, then backed away slowly from the radio.

'You're sure that's it?' The voice came from behind. Matt swung around, peered into the darkness, at first unable to discern the features of the man who'd spoken.

'31 metre. DXJ. You can see for yourself.' Dixie looked in the direction of a low car seat on which the man, Murt Costigan, was sitting with his arms tightly folded. He drew his lower lip firmly over the upper one and glared at the ground. Unsure of what was going on, but surmising they were radio enthusiasts, Matt sat down at the edge of the seat. The springs twanged and squeaked. Dixie's hand shot out, tensing in a plea for quiet as the singer threatened to fade out of range again. In an attempt to silence the uncoiling seat springs Matt brought as much of his weight as he could to bear on them. 'Come back to Érin', located once again, warbled slowly to its sentimental end.

'If you have any sense you won't say anything about this.' Costigan tipped his head in the direction of the wireless.

'How do you mean?'

'You heard what I said.'

He's taking this very seriously, Matt thought, wondering if there was something peculiar going on, a notion that receded when a voice, clear as crystal, broke through the hiss.

'*Fáilte.*'

Dixie's face flexed into high alert, eyebrows arching and head nodding as if to say to Matt, *You're on.*

Matt's response was immediate. 'Welcome.' He spoke decisively, drew breath as the presenter began to speak. The broadcast, an account of the achievements of the German armies in Russia, was wholly in Irish, the work, Matt assumed, of someone who broadcast a local, Irish-language version of 'Germany Calling', the English-language German propaganda programme. A fleeting image of his brother Hugh, sitting beside the radio at home scoffing at the theatrically plummy voice of Lord Haw Haw, crossed his mind. Straight away, he identified the North Eastern accent of the presenter because it was so similar to that of a Donegal fellow, Rory McShane, with whom he'd been friendly at the training college. The inflections, however, were exaggerated, many of them dramatized to create the impression that something of immense significance was about to follow. Matt pitched his translation accordingly, and for the first few minutes bounded along like a racing commentator, unwittingly galloping towards a revelation which, it became more and more obvious, wasn't going to materialize. Convinced that he ought to have put a calmer spin on it from the beginning, he hurriedly went back over the section he'd just translated, toning it down, trying, in the same breath, to explain what he was doing. He began to fall behind. The presenter, after holding forth at length about the heroism of the German armies in meeting the challenge of what he referred to as '*an bhagairt Sóibhéideach*', the Soviet threat, was now giving a detailed analysis of the difficulties facing those armies in Stalingrad. The information kept coming. In desperation, Matt started to skip bits. Soon he was doing little more than taking intermittent stabs at the broadcast, rattling along like a faulty engine, about to snarl to a halt.

'I think I'd be better off just listening, then going over it afterwards,' he gasped, taking hold of an imaginary pen, scribbling in the air, a gesture Dixie slowly registered as a request for pen and paper. He looked about the workshop, shook his head.

'The Russians …' Matt began when the broadcast ended, bracing himself to offer a quick, face-saving synopsis, while moving to the edge of the seat preparing to leave.

'No one gives a fuck about the Russians. Was there anything said about here?' Costigan repositioned himself aggressively, further tightening his already tightly folded arms.

'About here?' Matt repeated.

'Danny Boy' came and went woozily, then wobbled back for a few seconds before disappearing altogether. Dixie sidled up to the radio, for all the world a priest in the darkness of the confessional, ear pressed to the grille.

'That's what I said. About *here.*'

'About Rathisland?'

Costigan looked at Matt, sizing him up and down before he spoke.

'About here. Here.' He pointed to the ground then swung around and glared into the impenetrably dark corner to the right.

'Look. If you want to know, I haven't a clue what's going on. Mr Carmody asked me to help him out. Translate something from the wireless.' Matt swung around to face him directly. 'He had to meet a train. I thought it was going to be a match.'

Dixie laughed.

Costigan unfolded his arms; 'What I'm asking is, if *here*, if this country, came into it?' He pointed to the ground again. 'Was anything to do with *here* said?'

'No,' Matt said emphatically, standing up to leave.

'That's all I wanted to know.' Costigan nodded in a resigned, vaguely apologetic sort of way, his attention turning to the wireless when in a loud, clear voice a new presenter said, 'Flashback,' then continued after a brief pause. 'Exactly twenty-two years ago today the English authorities in Dublin Castle abolished the holding of coroner's inquests in ten counties, and introduced instead secret military courts of enquiry ...'

Relieved that the broadcast was no longer in Irish, Matt picked his way carefully to the pool of light fanning out from the open door, fielding a rush of questions about it all. He tried to think of something he might say that would place things on an even keel before he left.

'Call in any evening you're passing. Maybe there'll be a match.' Dixie pointed at the radio, guffawing loudly as though trying to draw Costigan into the joke.

'You never know,' Matt smiled, stepping into the yard. He had no intention whatsoever of returning.

The lemony September sunlight stung his eyes as he emerged. He bunched his fists to rub them, beginning to wonder if the anti-British broadcast he'd just translated was, as he had initially assumed, just the work of a local radio enthusiast. The suspicion that it could be part of something bigger had only begun to dawn on him when an image of Carmody's awe-struck response to his recital of 'Tír na nÓg' flashed to the fore. His head began to pound with the sound of his own voice reciting that poem, each elaborately pronounced syllable driving home the realization that he had been duped by Carmody into doing a translation of what was undoubtedly a politically shady broadcast. 'Fucker,' he said aloud, as the danger to which Carmody had exposed him hit home.

In an effort to rid himself of the smell of sump oil that had lodged somewhere at the back of his palate, he inhaled deeply, diverted from the questions plaguing him by a familiar scent, a scent he couldn't identify, but which grew sharper and at the same time sweeter in the clear air. Searching for its source, he turned and looked back towards the yard, fixed for a moment on the house, on the tangle of honeysuckle haphazardly bunched by string and attached to the front door surround. But the scent had a sourish tang. Not honeysuckle he thought, aware, as he continued to track it down, of movement at the periphery of his vision. Far away, in the small section of the cornfield visible from where he was standing, someone seemed to be waving. It was difficult to make out, impressionistic, a soft blend of colours, framed on one side by the crumbling, lean-to glasshouse and on the other by the gable end of the house. He took a few steps forward to get a clearer view, trying to establish if he was mistaken in thinking that the person under the spreading trees in the middle of the field was in fact waving at him. The scent now lingering on the precipice of recognition momentarily became that of stewing apples, disappearing before he could be sure. He saw that there were other people, two others, one on either side of the waving figure, both seated at a table, the whole scene shimmering in the ripples of latticed, pinkish light cast by the trees. Moving slowly back down towards the yard, as though hypnotically drawn, Matt could see that the figure, a tall, dark-haired girl, was not so much waving as beckoning him forward, slowly scooping the air in large, round armfuls.

The short stretch between the glasshouse and the gable end, leading from the yard into the field, was partly cobbled and marked out by two deep, parallel furrows hewn by carts and machinery. Matt didn't notice that some of the cobbled stones had been upturned, at least not until he'd tripped on one and stumbled forward, cascading into the cornfield like a drunkard. The corn had been recently cut, the stubble still sharp and unyielding underfoot. As he approached he thought they were eating, maybe having tea outside, but soon saw that the two seated figures were peeling and chopping at a table. The girl, younger than he thought – eighteen, maybe nineteen – standing arms akimbo and head to one side was observing his picky progress across the stubble.

'He's come to convert us all,' she proclaimed, wide-eyed, as he came into earshot, then pirouetted around, her dress swinging out as she considered the response of the two others to her announcement.

Matt didn't know what she meant, but smiled nonetheless. She pointed impatiently to the dictionary clasped under his arm, and, imitating Hattie McDaniel as Mammy in *Gone with the Wind*, said, 'A bible. Well I *do* dee-clare.'

'It's not a bible. It's a dictionary,' he said defensively, wishing, even as he spoke, that he'd said something else, something that didn't reveal how awkward he felt standing there with a big tome under his arm.

The nearer of the two women, a pale, mallow-skinned,

silvery blonde in her early forties, as unlikely a figure as anyone could have imagined meeting in the middle of that field, stood up, placed one hand delicately on her breastbone, then put down the large kitchen knife she was holding.

'You're the new teacher, Mr Duggan.' She held out her hand as though she were offering a precious object and smiled. 'Statia. Statia Coll.' She gestured in the direction of the other woman: 'My sister, Rose,' then searching, it appeared, for the appropriate way to introduce the unflinchingly expectant girl, 'Our niece, Madelene.' She smiled at Madelene.

Rose, though older-looking than Statia, had the same slightly stone-washed appearance. She nodded demurely. Madelene, still in *Gone with the Wind* mode, curtseyed, bobbing up to say, 'Why, my pleasure, I do bee-lieve,' revealing an arc of dazzling white teeth.

'I brought a dictionary. It was for translating. Dixie ...' He tossed his head in the direction of the yard, '... wanted something from the radio translated and asked Mr Carmody, who wasn't able to come because ...'

'I'm afraid you're mistaken. Very mistaken,' Rose said sharply, staring at Statia as she spoke. 'Dixie did not ask Mr Carmody to do anything. He is merely obliging that fellow from the town.'

'Mr Costigan. Murt Costigan,' Statia added, smiling as though to offset the disdain with which Rose had referred to him.

No one spoke for a moment.

'Dixie, you see, is an expert,' Statia said to Matt. 'Gets programmes on that wireless from all over the world.' Her face lit up, registering a mix of admiration and affection.

'Yes, he has a shortwave aerial,' Madelene spoke rapidly, 'but who wants to listen to the radio in a dark, filthy shed?' She crinkled her nose.

Statia laughed, Rose too, though not as wholeheartedly, both focusing on Matt in the expectation that he too should find it funny. He chuckled uneasily, overwhelmed by the peculiar sensation that everything he was thinking, every single thought, was apparent to Madelene.

Behind them, in a grassy, light-filled clearing was a fire, on top of which was a slushy mix of chopped apples bubbling furiously in a brass-handled, copper saucepan. An old washstand stood beside it and hanging, udder-like, through the open circle originally designed to contain a basin, was a straining bag of boiled apples. Thick, viscous juice dripped directly into an enamel bucket underneath.

'We heard you singing.'

'When?' Matt asked, registering for the first time that Madelene had an English accent.

'Yesterday, when we were passing by the school.' She drew breath, poised to continue, when Statia cut in.

'We don't know if it was him or not.' She smiled at Matt.

'It wasn't,' he said emphatically.

'The windows were wide open. We saw in. You were …'

'No. It must have been one of the other teachers.' He shook his head doggedly. He wanted the exchange with Madelene to end. He wanted to avoid looking at her at all costs in case the urgent, unfamiliar, lightning shafts bolting through him somehow burst out and registered on his face.

'We haven't been able to get over here all summer', Statia began, pausing, then continuing with a series of delicately choreographed gestures, backed up by the occasional, strategic word, *corn*, *trample*. The rush of confidence that had allowed her to take command and make those formal introductions in the opening moments of Matt's arrival had deserted her. Rose was quick to intervene.

'Never been corn here before. Takes a bit of getting used to.'

'I'd say it does. Some can't manage it at all.' Matt nodded, pleased to hear his voice sound so normal, to show that he was familiar with the controversy surrounding the statutory scheme, introduced the previous year, requiring landowners to make up for the wartime shortfall in grain imports by growing a designated amount.

'Yes,' Rose said indignantly, creating the impression that she had views on the scheme, definite views which she was about to disclose, but nothing followed.

'Yes,' Statia then exclaimed, striking the exact same note as if the conversation baton had unexpectedly landed on her lap. 'Yes, the government.' She grew alarmed, looked to Madelene who was now staring sullenly at Matt. He wanted desperately to row back, to arrive in the careless spirit in which he had been summoned, to reply to Madelene's playful welcome with some Rhett Butler riposte. He wanted to say *YES, you heard me singing*, maybe even sing a bar or two of the national anthem. All at once he became visible to himself through Madelene's eyes: he was humourless, chippy, defensive. He was wearing a thick pullover and a jacket, even though it was a warm September evening. He was carrying a large, Irish-English dictionary. He was too big. He was speaking to her aunts about the government. He was sweating. Fearful that any attempt to change tack at this stage would just backfire, he pointed to the old, flaking washstand.

'A clever way of doing the straining.' Words he plied with fascination, but which came across as forced.

'Dixie's invention,' Statia said indulgently, taking up the chopping knife as she spoke.

'Very clever at everything,' Rose added. Then, as though mysteriously summoned by the mention of his name, Dixie's voice calling Madelene from the gable end of the house.

She took off across the field, raising her hand and waving hastily as she went. Matt watched her quickening pace, her hair rising and falling in what seemed like slow motion.

The conversation with Rose and Statia dribbled slowly into generalities about the war, 'the duration' as they referred to it. Matt was barely present, agreeing and disagreeing as the rhythm dictated, all the time thinking of circumstances under which he could return. His thoughts raced around at blinding speed as one new plan, one new way of returning, replaced another, each wholly plausible one moment, absurd the next. And all around, frantically meshing the silvery evening light as he made his way across the field were millions of midges, locked into a furious dance to the death.

At the top of the lane, seized by a sudden impulse, he swung around, certain that Madelene was watching him leave. And for an immeasurably small splint of time, she was. She was there, a figure waving, beckoning him towards her just as she'd done in the cornfield, an image so potent that it had remained stamped on his retina, only disappearing when everything surrounding it, the outhouse gable, the wilting foxgloves, the tangle of sloe bushes conspired to impress on him that it was an illusion. And even then, the space where he imagined she'd stood, took on the aura of her absence, prompting him to dally at the top of the lane, his squinched eyes widening, his face slowly slacking as he began to regain possession of himself.

He strode along under the colonnade of chestnut trees lining the road back to the town, going out of his way to avoid stepping on the dark patches, skipping from one pool of light to the next, stopping occasionally to chart the route forward through the shimmering deltas that stretched ahead. Navigating those pools of light quickly became a game to divine his future with Madelene, a game he modified as he leapt from one to the next, tempering his tearaway success by introducing new, more difficult rules as he went, imposing strictures that would make the journey forward almost impossible, when a little distance ahead, he heard a branch snap. Then a burst of children's voices, accusations, harshly whispered, soon to fall silent as he passed beneath. Scattered in the dappled shade of the tree were dozens of spiky chestnut shells, broken open. He glanced up, unsure of what he should say if they turned out to be pupils, relieved that he couldn't see them through the dense foliage, swallowing hard and shutting his eyes tightly when it struck him that that they might have seen him dancing his way through the pools of light, waltzing alone on the Castle Wall Road. Once a few paces beyond, those voices took up again, furtive at first, growing louder behind him then thinning gradually, soon to become nothing more than a brief respite from planning how he could meet Madelene again.

Chapter 5

When Matt arrived back Mrs Sheridan was sitting at the dining-room table totting up golf scores. She was wearing glasses; big, ill-fitting glasses with heavy tortoiseshell frames. She tipped them upwards, explaining that they'd belonged to her husband, Benny.

'He was so fast at adding, could do it just by looking.' She pointed to the mound of score cards and sighed. Matt stood in the doorway, eager to find out if she knew the Colls, if she could tell him anything, anything at all about Madelene. Mentioning the broadcast was out of the question. What if she decided to report it? He imagined her looking earnestly at him, explaining that she felt honour-bound to inform Sergeant Cotton. Even thinking about it angered him. It brought Carmody to mind, standing beside him in the classroom, encouraging his foolishly exaggerated recital of the poem.

'I went for a walk out the Castle Wall Road.'

'Glorious evening.' Her eyes flickered to a close as she spoke.

'Met a family called Coll. Two sisters,' he paused, then casually added, 'And their niece, Madelene.'

'Oh yes.' She smiled, 'Statia and Rose Coll.'

Matt gazed round the room in a distracted sort of way, trying to create the impression that whatever she might say about them was of little or no consequence. But she said nothing at all, just continued totting. The rank smell of boiled nettles, one of the ingredients of a soup Mrs Sheridan had been preparing earlier for her 'making do' class in the technical school, lingered in the room.

'D'you know them?' He asked after a moment or two.

'A little. Through Benny mostly.' Her grip on her pencil loosened, causing it to tilt to one side. 'He knew them at the business end. In the bank. Did everything he could for them, but their brother, what's-his-name, just didn't …'

'Dixie,' Matt said as she spoke.

'Dixie, just didn't have a business head. Within a year of taking over from old Mr Coll the debts at the foundry had mounted beyond the beyond …' She raised her hand up from the table, conjuring a big stack of money, 'there was no choice but to sell. He wasn't interested. Wasn't interested in anything but cars.'

'The foundry? They owned that big …' Matt pointed in the direction of the foundry which he passed on his way to and from the school.

'Yes. And a bakery. And goodness knows what else. Years ago. A farm too. They still have that, though Dixie …' She smiled in a vaguely compassionate sort of way, a display of restraint, a tacit reminder to Matt that she was privy to information that was confidential.

'Nice neck of the woods,' Matt said speculatively, trying at the same time to figure how he could question her further without revealing how interested he was.

'The Castle Wall Road, yes, many's the evening Benny and I walked it, did the round, coming back by Lisnahincha bridge.'

'They seemed, I don't know, unusual?' he persisted.

'Benny always said they were exceptionally courteous.'

Courteous, Matt thought, searching the word for implications, Madelene's voice suddenly ringing in his ears, *A bible. Well I do dee-clare.* Her hands on her hips, her laughter taunting, a carelessness about her.

'And friendly. Madelene was …'

'I've never actually met their niece.' She picked up a score card, ran her pencil up the margin as she totted, then almost as though she was talking to herself, added, 'But I've often seen her with them, quite a looker.'

'Yes,' Matt replied, swallowing hard, certain he detected some sort of reservation, maybe even hostility.

'Extraordinary the number of people who don't fill in their handicap. As though I should know it off the top of my head.' She shook her head, reached for the membership list.

'Does she live with them?'

'I gather she came here last year when the raids began again.' She scrutinized Matt from over the rim of her husband's glasses, then resumed totting in a fussy, exasperated whisper.

'From England?'

'Yes. Larry, her father, was quite the man about town when Benny and I first arrived. Then there was some sort of family disagreement. Next thing we … Benny heard he'd joined the army. Benny always said he had a great flair for business, would never have let things go the way they went.'

'The army?' Matt asked, unsure if she meant the British or the Irish army.

'Yes. Or was it the RAF? I don't recall. Anyway, it was all downhill from then. Very hard on Statia. Rose too. People just arrived into the farmyard and helped themselves to this and that. Told Dixie they were borrowing them but never brought them back. Sad, very sad.'

Mrs Sheridan shook her head, as if to admonish herself for getting sidetracked from her work and with that she picked up a score card and, almost scowling with concentration, began to tot.

'Do they visit her? I mean Madelene's parents?'

'I couldn't say. I …' She paused, began to tot again. It was a further bid to impress on Matt that she wasn't at liberty to talk about people who had been clients of her late husband. Matt, however, saw it as a deliberate attempt to withhold something about Madelene.

'Do they come into the town? Shopping or that?'

Mrs Sheridan didn't look up, but raised her finger a little, indicating that she was in the middle of adding up a score and would answer as soon as she had finished. A moment or two later, she shook her head, seemingly convinced by the result she got that she'd made an error. She began again.

'I suppose they must,' Matt eventually said, reluctantly accepting that he had learned as much as he was going to learn.

'I'll be off.'

'Sleep well.'

As soon as Matt was out in the hall he began to piece together everything he'd learned about Madelene, assembling and reassembling the details, poring over them with all the concentration of a gold panner.

He lay awake mulling over those details, creating a future for her in which he would be the mainstay, all the while conjuring one new self after another, each fashioned to eclipse the humourless, dictionary-carrying self that had stumbled into the cornfield a few hours earlier.

*Yes I have come to convert you. Step this way. Right up
here.* He points to the space directly in front of him. Imagines
Madelene laughing, bouncing forward. She bows her head
a little. Her shoulders tense as he places his hands on them,
softening when he draws her towards him. He raises his
hands, cups them gently around her head, holds her cheeks
in his palms. Her arms fold around him, tighten, tighten
further: then just as they begin to dissolve into each other,
he bolts up, rearranges his pillow, begins again. *Yes I have
come to convert you. Step this way. Right up here.* He proceeds
more slowly this time, savouring every move, each breath
longingly drawn, drunk on the mix of fear and pleasure.

The following morning he woke with a childlike sense
of expectancy, a feeling that there was some great event
pending, something he'd been looking forward to for a long
time. Slowly, Madelene came into focus, a vision suffused
with the sweet, sharp scent of apples cooking and the chaffy
aftermath of cut corn: a vision no sooner formed than it
vanished, violently supplanted by the fear that he might not
get a second chance, that he'd made such a poor impression
in the cornfield she'd written him off there and then. He
decided to go directly to her house, a plan he instantly abandoned when he glimpsed himself standing at Colls' front
door, facing Madelene, unable to speak, and so compoun-
ding the poor impression he'd made the previous evening.
He was so preoccupied by these thoughts that he didn't
immediately see the significance of Mrs Sheridan's get up.
She was wearing a white, knee-length pleated skirt, a white
linen blouse and plimsolls. The edges of the pleats were razor
sharp, all of them slightly yellowing from the same point
downwards, indicating that the skirt had been stored away
for a long time. The laces of her plimsolls, though white, were
less brilliantly so than the shoes themselves which had been

whitened to such an extent that her legs appeared grey.

All week Matt had regretted agreeing to play in the match against Abbeyleix. He'd scarcely ever held a racquet and furthermore when, in the hope of borrowing one, he'd mentioned the arrangement to Canning, Canning had laughed loudly, then even louder when Matt had asked him why he was laughing.

'Who's playing?' Matt asked Mrs Sheridan when it occurred to him that Madelene could be there.

'Depends really on who turns up. Wilkie Hodgins and Helen Stanley are the most reliable. I've asked the new bank clerk, whose name I've been trying to recall all morning. One or two others, Nuala Gilmartin, Mary Lowrey, and of course, Rowena. Rowena Harrington.' Her forehead crinkled as she searched for other names.

'The Colls?' Matt blurted out.'

'No. No.' She shook her head decisively, then seemed to check herself. 'No. I mean, Rose and Statia used to play years ago, but they don't mix much now. Hardly at all, really. Anyway, they're not members. They decided not to join.'

Matt's apprehension about playing returned in force.

'I don't have a racquet,' he announced, knowing it was a difficulty she would overcome, but at the same time hoping he might be let off the hook. Mrs Sheridan went into the hall and returned with a racquet in a wooden press, the one he'd pointed out on his first afternoon.

'Bit on the small side, but it should be alright.' She was cheerful, reassuring.

Written on the press in neat, round letters was *Evelyn Sheridan, Loretto College, St Stephen's Green, Dublin.* Matt stared at the words, not out of curiosity, at least not primarily so, but in a bid to make time while he tried to work out how to open the press.

'Evelyn, it belongs to my daughter Evelyn,' she said after observing him read the inscription for a moment or two.

He released the springs and manoeuvred the racquet out, puzzled that Mrs Sheridan, who had mentioned her husband so often in the course of that first week, had not at any stage mentioned her daughter.

'Evelyn is studying abroad,' she then said formally, adding, 'at the conservatoire in Basel.'

It seemed so grandiose. Matt wasn't sure how to respond, so he just said, 'The conservatoire in Basel?'

'The piano.' She gestured theatrically towards the drawing room, to the baby grand, giving him time to piece it all together. He imagined a very serious girl, doggedly practising scales in a large, furnitureless room overlooking a lake. He then recalled a letter, among others he'd picked up off the floor and left on the hall stand earlier that week. It had been opened by the censors, a fact acknowledged by a large sticker resealing the envelope and readily explained by the Swiss stamp.

The existence of a daughter, Evelyn, didn't tally with the impression Matt had formed of Mrs Sheridan as being more or less alone in the world. Suddenly she seemed less familiar, more private than he'd supposed. However, there wasn't time to think about that, what with the half-dozen assorted bottles of cloudy lemonade and the two dented, USA biscuit tins of hardboiled egg sandwiches to be brought to the tennis club, the second court still to be relined, the Burco water boiler to be collected from the parochial hall, the nets to be raised, the pavilion to be opened up, all before the arrival of the Abbeyleix team.

As it turned out, it wasn't a match at all, at least not a match in the competitive sense. Teams were made up from the assembled group, with players selected regardless of whether they were from Rathisland or Abbeyleix. In a way everyone won, because victory lay in turning up, in just being there. This became clear the moment the Abbeyleix group, led by Wilkie Hodgins, arrived. They were all considerably older that Matt. Wilkie Hodgins was in his early forties and Rowena Harrington was a decade older, if not more. They had cycled twelve miles, the two younger ones, Mary Lowrey and Nuala Gilmartin, on the same High Nellie, laughing, falling off as they made their way up the last stretch of the deeply pitted, dusty lane leading to the courts. The pavilion, as Mrs Sheridan referred to it, was a forlorn building with a flaking red, corrugated-iron roof and no windows. But when the four heavy wooden shutters were extended outwards and hooked up to form a low awning, it took on something of the appearance of a seaside shop opened for the summer season. Four foldable card tables were placed under this awning and the refreshments, including a marble cake and a mound of butterfly buns brought by the Abbeyleix team, laid out in the deep shade it provided. The changing rooms, two dry toilets to the right and left of the pavilion, identified as *Ladies* and *Gents* by hastily handwritten signs tacked up by Mrs Sheridan, were entered from the rear of the building. The buzz of zigzagging flies in the Gents created a tropical, feverish torpor. It took Matt several moments to realize that they were in a crazed state, hurling themselves blindly against the sealed skylight, dying from the fumes of whatever noxious chemical had been poured on the lime in the toilet pits shortly beforehand.

Matt had taken an irrational dislike to Wilkie Hodgins before he met him, based on the name *Wilkie*. This was compounded by the number of times everyone used his name in the half-hour or so before the games got underway. Wilkie this, Wilkie that, loudly incorporating it into practically every sentence that passed between them. It was as though the name was a rallying call, a catch cry used to muster intimacy among a group who, despite the rapid flow of talk, were not at ease with each other. At any rate, whatever purpose that name served, Matt found it very irksome. So when he was selected to play with him in a doubles match against Rowena Harrington and Mary Gilmartin, he was little more than tacitly courteous.

'I've never played before,' he said laconically.

'That's alright. There's a first time for everything,' Wilkie smiled blandly then with a quick flick, tossed the flat strands of thinning fair hair off his forehead.

Once the game started Matt saw that Wilkie was going out of his way to make sure he didn't feel like a novice. Whenever he returned a ball Wilkie was quick to say 'Well done' and he pretended not to notice when, on a number of occasions, Matt called the court 'the pitch'. If an easy ball came their way, which it frequently did from Mary Gilmartin, he stepped aside and encouraged Matt to return it.

'You have a powerful overarm,' he told Matt after the first set, then went on to explain that his returns would be more accurate, would stand a better chance of being in if he held the racquet with one hand. He gave a short demonstration, swiping his racquet this way and that, holding it first with two hands, then with one.

'Of course there are times when two hands make for a real whammer.' He smiled.

Unlike Wilkie Hodgins, Rowena Harrington was uncompromising. Using as much tennis jargon as she could, she took every opportunity to point out the rules. The few compliments she did voice were essentially self-serving in that they highlighted her own ability to identify some particular tactic or other.

'Splendid topspin,' she hollered so loudly at one point that play came to a momentary standstill on the other court.

'Just lucky,' Wilkie replied jauntily, then turning to Matt, raised his eyebrows and smiled a little, letting him know that even though he was friendly with Rowena he did not wish to be associated with her arrogant, overbearing carry on. Both he and Rowena belonged to the same, dwindling Church of Ireland community and were bound together in their commitment to its continuance. Supporting the tennis club was a statement of that commitment. Turning up for matches was in some ways on a par with turning up for church. But, as was very apparent that afternoon, Wilkie and Rowena approached the challenges to their way of life in very different ways. Rowena took it upon herself to uphold the rules at every turn while Wilkie recognized that ultimately there would be no need for rules, there would be no game, no club, no tennis unless potentially new members like Matt were successfully initiated. This he did with ease and charm, so it came as a bit of a surprise to Matt to find afterwards at tea that there was something restless, even gloomy about him. He stood at a slight distance, cup and saucer in hand, looking across the courts and through the high wire fence to the flat, burnished moorland and the cloudy mountains beyond. When Matt went over and thanked him, he smiled, told him he'd played well for a beginner, then almost immediately directed his sights back to the distant horizon, his face tensing. Had he, Matt wondered, just acquitted himself well on the court out of a sense of duty? Loyalty to the club? Would he have preferred to be elsewhere? At home farming? Or at war, where as Matt would later learn from Mrs Sheridan, his uncle was in command of an entire regiment.

Chapter 6

'No, I'm full, thanks. I ate so much after the tennis, all the buns and stuff, it'd be just wasted. I'm off for a walk. Maybe when I come back.'

'You're sure? A boiled egg would be ready in a jiffy.'

'No thanks.' Matt shoved Evelyn's tennis racquet in between the umbrellas and bounded up the stairs, two steps at a time. Rummaging through the still partially unpacked bag, he hurriedly pulled out his good shirt.

Downstairs, unaware that he was preparing to go to Colls Mrs Sheridan listened, puzzling over the pounding footsteps above, the bathroom door thrown open and slammed shut, the whole house reverberating with the clatter of washing and scrubbing. Then, minutes later, Matt's flight downstairs, a short drumroll followed by a loud clap as he bounced onto the hall floor.

'I'm leaving the sandwiches, just the ham ones, in the tin. The rest is in the Fly-tight.' Words that trailed after Matt as he rushed down the hall, rippling the air with the whiff of Brylcreem.

'I'm leaving the sandwiches …' Mrs Sheridan began again, stepping into the hall, but he was already gone, leaving a fragile, battered silence, like that in a country railway station after a train has sped through.

Out on the Castle Wall Road the overhanging chestnut trees formed a series of dark tunnels alive with birdsong, leading to oases of light, each quivering in the tinselly September sunshine. The energy to break into a gallop kept welling inside him, constantly on the point of spilling over, contained only by the thought that he would be seen, seen running to Colls, hair sleeked and laboriously parted, shirt sleeves folded and rolled like starched napkins, face glowing with expectation.

Once onto the lane, he could no longer sustain a walking pace and began to trot. The cattle at the far side of the hedge pounded across the field as they had done the evening before, creating a backdrop to the panicky scarper of birds through the dark inner reaches of the hedgerows. And delicately above that, a sound he hadn't heard before and didn't identify until he was almost in the yard – the crackle of foxglove pods, their seeds scattering like milled pepper on the foliage all around.

A sharp tapping noise sounded from beneath the raised bonnet of a cream Hillman parked over beside the pump. Dixie, who was leaning in and over the engine, stood up and backed a few paces from the car as Matt approached. He was older than Matt had supposed in the darkness of the outhouse the previous evening, but at the same time boyish, a shock of tussled black curly hair perched on one side of his head like an ill-fitting wig.

'A bit of repair work?' Matt nodded in the direction of the open bonnet, wondering what he could be doing when there was no fuel available.

'Ah no. No, just …' He shrugged his shoulders, took a mottled rag from the pocket of his oil-caked overalls, wiped his hands. 'Just making sure it doesn't seize up, not running and that.'

'I was passing by.' Matt laughed a little. 'Wondered if there was anything going on …' Laughed a little more.

Dixie looked puzzled.

'I'd make a better stab at it, better than last night at any rate, if there was something, you know, to be translated.' Matt had hardly finished speaking when he was seized by an impulse to unsay what he'd just said.

Dixie's face flinched with concern. 'Costigan never said anything about coming this evening.'

'I just thought …' Matt rolled his head carelessly from side to side, trying to create the impression that he was there on a whim. He glanced across the yard to the cornfield gate and beyond to the trees in the middle of the field, sights fixed on the empty space beneath. And he continued to look, prompted by the senseless hope that it would suddenly unfurl into the scene it was the evening before, Madelene in her round-necked, peppermint-coloured frock, beckoning him over.

'But you can never tell with him, never tell when he's going to show up.' He threw his head back with an air of abandonment.

Alerted by the rattle of a bicycle Matt and Dixie looked over towards the lane just as a man, not much older than Matt, sped into the yard, trying without much success to weave his way around the bumps and potholes. In a single, slickly co-ordinated movement, he leapt off the bike and flung it against the straw-lagged pump. He glanced hurriedly in Matt's direction before he spoke to Dixie.

'Is the trap yoked up?' His bicycle-clipped trousers flapped like pantaloons as he approached.

'If I'd known you wanted it …'

'You're not using it?' The man cut in impatiently.

Dixie assured him he wasn't.

'Well then, come on. We'll round up the old pony.'

Matt's attention turned to the house. He thought he saw a figure moving past a partially opened window, forced to acknowledge, after gazing at it for a moment or two, that it was only a shadow cast by the curtains. He began to edge his way over, determined to place himself in a position where he would be seen if anyone looked out.

Nobody did.

Observed by Dixie, now leading the pony in from the paddock, he made his way up to the front door, about to knock when Dixie's high-pitched voice sounded across the yard.

'No one in there.'

Matt froze as though discovered doing something sneaky, a feeling that momentarily gave way to a sense of relief.

'They've gone for a walk.'

He dawdled on the step.

'I'll call some other time.' He spoke as casually as he could, already heading for the lane, weighing up his chances of catching up with them.

Once at the top of the lane he turned right, the opposite direction to the town. The road, although a direct continuation of the Castle Wall Road, became much narrower at that point and was no longer formally lined with trees. He broke into a trot, slowing down as he approached each twist, drawing breath, straightening his collar, running his hand across his hair, preparing for the encounter which he hoped was just about to take place when he turned the corner. Now and then he imagined he heard voices ahead, but whenever he stopped to listen, they just trickled away into the stillness of the evening. The waft of dampening foliage, of overripe cow parsley mixed with a fungal, mushroomy smell deepened as the hedgerow banks drew closer. And on he rushed, on and on, streaks of white evening light strobing through the sloe thickets, the night closing solemnly around him, the ever lengthening trek back to Rathisland gradually sapping his will to continue. It was pitch dark when, exasperated by his failure, he decided to turn and head back to the town.

The following day, all Matt's hopes were fixed on meeting Madelene at Mass. Arriving early and positioning himself beside a large marbled pillar towards the back of the church, he carefully monitored the arrival of the rest of the congregation. When she did not walk up the central aisle with her aunts, as he expected her to do every second, he figured she must have come in the side door and slipped into one of the back pews. Turning around casually, his eyes darting busily from side to side, he scanned the half-dozen or so rows directly behind him. A moment or two later, he conducted a similar search of the pews at the other side of the aisle, forced, when he didn't find her there, to accept that she wasn't in the church, that she must have been at the earlier Mass.

Little by little he abandoned himself to the familiar, sing-song lilt of the Mass, vacantly following the rhythmic way Father Finn spun from the missal to the tabernacle, his hands held up. Random thoughts came and went, some spinning themselves into daydreams; reveries he shook off with a shrug as he tried to appear devout, to behave as he felt the people of Rathisland expected a teacher to. These efforts brought him back to the church in Balbriggan, to a time when his mother, kneeling upright beside him, would turn her head towards him without moving the rest of her body and urgently whisper any one of a series of directives: *don't slouch, kneel up straight and follow the Mass, don't fidget ...*

Wandering from daydream to liturgy, liturgy to daydream he continued to while away the Mass, until, out of the blue, just as Father Finn swung into the *Pater Noster*, it struck him that Madelene could be a Protestant. He almost said the word aloud, his head already spinning with the complications to which that would give rise. He began to weigh up the odds, her surname, Coll. It was the maiden name of de Valera's mother. It had to be Catholic. On the other hand, they'd once owned the foundry. And Dixie, Rose and Statia's house had a Protestant appearance, a Protestant feel to it. His thoughts fixed briefly on the big tangle of honeysuckle haphazardly bunched by string and attached to the hall door surround, then on the gleaming brass door knob and knocker. But Mrs Sheridan's brasses also gleamed and she was a Catholic. He tried to figure out if Statia was a Catholic or a Protestant name. He thought about Wilkie Hodgins and Rowena Harrington, whom he'd automatically identified as Protestants when Mrs Sheridan said their names in the kitchen the morning before. Playing tennis with them that afternoon was as close as he'd ever come to mixing socially with Protestants. The schools in Balbriggan, as elsewhere, were segregated. So too were a great many activities in which he might have come into direct contact with Protestants. He recalled that when some years earlier a statue to the Blessed Virgin was erected in a prominent place in the town to celebrate the Eucharistic Congress, a boy in his class, Tony O' Meara, had announced that 'it was a good slap in the puss for the Protestants'.

Once out of the church, he made his way as briskly as he could down Main Street, hardly able to wait to ask Mrs Sheridan, who'd been at the earlier Mass, what religion Madelene was. The full consequences of her being Protestant began to emerge in force. If it turned out to be true, which,

as his pace quickened to a trot, seemed more and more possible, he would just have to try and forget the whole thing.
However disapproving Father Finn might be, and he would,
if only in his role as school manager, be very disapproving,
Carmody, Matt felt, would be more so. Much more so. And
they were the ones who, the following July, would decide if
he'd satisfactorily completed his probationary year. Getting
involved with a Protestant girl was almost certain to stymie
his chances of success. He saw himself trying to explain his
failure to complete his probationary year satisfactorily to his
mother and his brothers, an image that almost brought him
to a standstill. He was altogether unfamiliar with the depths
to which these thoughts had dragged him. And he founde-
red around trying to find his bearings, deeply agitated by the
notion of having to turn his back on something he yearned
for more than he'd ever yearned for anything before.

Once inside the hall door he drew breath slowly, determined to be as calm as possible. *Not that peculiar*, he thought,
asking Mrs Sheridan if Madelene is a Protestant, but unable, all
the same, to settle on a satisfactory way of wording the question. He stood in the dining-room tossing the words this way
and that, waiting for her to come through from the kitchen.

It's hard to know with people ... Opening words he'd just
settled on when he saw a note, written on a small white, paper
bag, sitting on top of the metal plate cover on the table.

Won't be here for lunch. If I'm not back by suppertime there
are egg sandwiches etc. in the Fly-tight. Mrs H. Sheridan.

Mrs Sheridan had left a large salad, complete with beetroot, hard-boiled egg, thickly cut, sugar-edged slices of
ham, lettuce, scallions and radishes. Matt stared vacantly at
the food, picked up the note and read it again, scrutinizing
it as though it could contain some indication, some clue as
to how she might have answered the question he so urgently

wanted to ask. He threw it aside, picked up his knife and fork but was no sooner chewing his first mouthful, a mix of every item on his plate, when Mrs Sheridan's guarded, almost hostile responses to the questions he'd asked her about the Colls the other evening, loomed up. *That's it,* he thought, *that's it for certain, she was trying to warn me.* Madelene is definitely a Protestant. He tried to swallow but found his throat constricted. He craned his head forward, tried again, this time managing to force the partially chewed food down in a single, violent swallow.

The previous Wednesday at the end of morning break, Matt had mentioned to Canning that he could, if he felt like it, call to Mrs Sheridan's on Sunday afternoon and listen to the All-Ireland final, Cork v. Dublin, which they'd been discussing for the previous ten minutes or so.

'Ah no, no. I wouldn't, no, no.' Canning said so emphatically that Matt got the impression he shouldn't have asked.

'It's just if you wanted to listen to it in peace,' Matt said referring to a complaint Canning had made a few moments beforehand about missing the build-up to a decisive goal in the semi-final because of the racket his landlady's children were making.

'No, anyway I'll have the place to myself on Sunday. They're all going up the town to the grandfather to listen to it,' he'd said, words Matt now repeated to himself as he ran the side of his little finger across his plate scooping up the pieces of beetroot-sodden egg yolk, too small to get on to his fork. He raised his hand to his mouth, rapidly twisting it so as to lick the already dribbling juice from his finger, all the while coasting closer and closer to the notion of going to Canning's digs and, under the pretext of calling to listen to the match with him, find out if he knew whether or not the Colls were Protestants.

Canning's digs was one of a row of six small, single-storey houses on the narrow lane that led to the rear entrances of the houses and shops on Main Street. Matt was not sure which house it was but figured it must be the last one, or maybe the one before, because the previous Friday he'd seen Canning coming up from the bottom of the lane on his way to school. Once there, he found that the second-last house was derelict, or as good as, and so decided to knock on the last one.

Canning's small head appeared through the gap in the narrowly opened door, his expression framed to announce that there was no one in but himself. He looked at Matt for a few seconds, slow to register that he was the one being called on.

'Just thought we could listen to the match.' Matt smiled.

Canning stood back a little, then opened the door fully. 'Come in. You may as well, now that you're here.' He pointed to his feet. 'I take off me shoes and socks once I'm inside.' He laughed a little.

Matt might have laughed too, but was busily trying to conceal his response to the condition of the place. All that remained of the linoleum on the hall floor was a thin strip close to the wall on each side, with a few patches of the black underside stuck to the ground here and there. The rest had been worn away, exposing the concrete floor beneath. Most of the skirting boards had been pulled off, leaving a few jagged strips, bits too securely fixed to be prised off for what Matt figured was kindling. The smell of chemical toilet cleaner gave way periodically to a damp, vaguely fungal whiff, as Matt followed Canning down the dark hall.

'Cork are leading by four points,' Canning announced,

stepping down into a low scullery kitchen. High up on a partially painted shelf, a radio, turned up to maximum volume, filled the room with the familiar voice of Mícheál Ó hEithir. '*Ciúnas.*' Canning reached up, turned it down a little.

'I keep it loud to hear it from inside.' He gestured to the open door of a cell-like bedroom, which had three brightly coloured pictures taped to the far wall; St Francis of Assisi, Blessed Martin de Porres and Padré Pio. The faded mustard-coloured candlewick bedspread dipped in the centre, bearing the outline of Canning's shape.

'It's not Buckingham Palace.' He smiled. Ran the palm of his hand over his head. 'But you have to take into account that there's no rent, only the bit of work I do in the evenings with the young lads, getting them ready for the scholarships.'

'How many of them are there?'

'Six. Well, five now. The eldest fella, Con, landed himself a scholarship in the Presentations below in Cork.' Canning waved his hand dismissively, downplaying what he obviously regarded as his own success.

'That's fair going,' Matt nodded several times in quick succession, a display of admiration that might have got things onto an easier footing, had Canning not felt obliged to go on explaining his circumstances.

'It won't be forever. I have two brothers above in the Uni, one finishing veterinary next year, the other with two years to go in Ag.'

'No rent.' Words Matt tried to charge with disbelief, releasing his grip on the question he came to ask.

'You couldn't meet nicer people.' Canning looked to Matt for a response, his expression expectant but at the same time sheepishly apologetic. Matt wished he hadn't called, not so much because of the circumstances in which he found Canning living, a setup to which he could easily have adjusted, but because of the position into which he had put him, pushed to the pin of his collar explaining and apologizing.

'You know the woman of the house, Joan, who cleans the school,' Canning said in a rush, racing ahead to explain that her husband, Frank, worked in England, facts that just added to the discomfort Matt felt.

'Joan,' Matt exclaimed, 'you couldn't do better than Joan.'

The galloping pace of the commentator's voice signalled a dramatic development in the game, a shot at goal from midfielder Ned Wade. Canning pointed to the only seat in the room, a straight-backed chair wedged between the rickety wooden draining board and the gas cooker. Matt sat down, trying to avoid brushing against the long lines of solidified lard running down the side of the cooker. The faecal smell, which until then he'd been blocking out by breathing through his mouth, was now overpowering. Sensing he must be close to the source, he glanced down at the open space beneath the draining board to his right, quickly swinging away when he saw the cluster of blue flies circling the bucket of soiled nappies.

The plan to ask Canning if the Colls were Protestants was now totally out of reach. There was nothing for it except to listen to the match and leave as soon as it ended. When, eventually, that moment came he stood up, prompting Canning, who'd been sitting on the edge of his bed, twisting his large, knobbly toes into the frayed straw bedside mat, to stand up too.

'What's the story if a fella wanted to have a drink, I mean if you wanted to go for a pint some evening?' Matt asked half jokily, keen to make amends for the position into which he'd put him by calling.

Canning looked alarmed, but only for a split second. 'I

needn't tell you there'd be no question of a pub, unless of course you wanted a repeat of the Spanish Inquisition.' He laughed, confident that Matt was well aware of what Rathisland would and would not tolerate from teachers.

'It's that bad, is it?' Matt feigned an expression of despair.

'Well, you might get away with Dowlings, if there weren't too many around. On a week night, say.'

'Dowlings?'

'Yes, the Commercial Hotel.' Canning, now standing in the doorway pointed in the direction of the Square.

'Would you be on to give it a try some night?'

'Well sure, why not?'

'Maybe some evening next week?'

'We'd have to be careful, though. Everything is reported.'

Once back up on Main Street, silent and empty in the aftermath of the match, Madelene shot to the forefront of Matt's thoughts again. The obstacle posed by her being a Protestant seemed more insurmountable than ever. Mrs Sheridan is surely home by now, he thought, quickening his pace when he saw a pony and trap with three people pulling up outside the house. A youngish man leapt out and opened the trapdoor in a playful, extravagant sort of way, while Mrs Sheridan, assisted by him, made her way carefully onto the step, then equally carefully onto the street. All at once he didn't want the question about Madelene answered. There was hope while it remained unanswered, but the sickening possibility of hopelessness once it was.

'You got the note I left. It was all so last-minute.' Two sherries before lunch had flushed Mrs Sheridan's cheeks and made her movements fussy and impatient.

'It was grand. Thanks.'

'I really didn't know what to say when Una Hayse sidled up to me after Mass. Such short notice, but Paul, her husband was such a close friend of Benny's. I felt I ought to, if even just for his sake. And when they said they'd send Dennis, their son to collect me, I …'

'No it was fine. Anyway I'm well able to manage by myself.' Matt spoke slowly, all his resources deployed to contain the urge he felt to ask the question, at least until she had taken her hat and coat off.

'Dennis did medicine. He's just qualified and is talking about joining up, which has Una in a state. Naturally. Thinking, as any mother would …' She stopped suddenly, dabbed her hair firmly with her hand, a gesture intended to convey that she knew she was prattling on about people Matt didn't know.

'Are the Colls Catholic or Protestant?' The question just burst through the fences corralling it, wholly under its own steam, gathering so much momentum that it emerged more as a demand than the casual enquiry Matt was planning.

'Oh goodness. Catholic, of course.' Mrs Sheridan's eyes narrowed as she looked up at Matt. In another country, in another time he might have flung his arms around her, lifted her off the ground, swung her around, but self-control was the order of the day so he just stood there, trying to think of something to say. Anything. Anything at all just as long as it sounded normal.

'It's just that I didn't see them at Mass.'

Mrs Sheridan – suddenly attuned to why he wanted to know – looked across at the photograph of Benny on the mantelpiece, turning to him as if for guidance.

'I suppose if the truth were told they don't always go to Mass.' She cast her eyes down as though she had been forced to disclose something she would have rather kept to herself, then looked up boldly, confident that she had placed an obstacle on Matt's path. It had the opposite effect. It confirmed his impression that Madelene was free-spirited, on for adventure. He wanted to race away with these thoughts, take fuller possession of them, revel in the knowledge that she wasn't a Protestant, a thought that kept returning in heady, exuberant waves, spilling right over into a surge of affection for Mrs Sheridan, bearer of the good news.

'I know how lucky I am here.'

Taken by surprise, Mrs Sheridan was quick to rally, though not before Matt had begun to explain what he meant.

'With the food and all.' He nodded in the direction of the kitchen, recalling the squalid conditions in which Canning was living.

'That's nice of you to say so. Matthew. Very nice.' Her face softened as she abandoned herself to the enjoyment she always found in good manners.

'Well, it's the truth,' Matt said emphatically.

That truth, by very virtue of being stated became an even greater truth in the days and weeks that followed, with Mrs Sheridan making more elaborate, more diverse, ever larger suppers. In addition, she insisted on taking over the preparation of a packed lunch for school, something Matt had, until now, done himself.

Chapter 7

Every morning at eight Rathisland was shaken into life by the rapid, urgent clanging of the foundry bell. The works, as the place was called, had been contracted shortly before Matt's arrival to supply the newly established national shipping company with sheet iron. This marked a welcome upturn in its fortunes. The heavy metal gate groaned open as the bell tolled, and the shifting clusters of peak-capped boys and men, billycans swinging by their sides, sloped down to the foundry yard. The whole place was in full swing, hammers pounding, carts rolling and the furnace chimney billowing great spumes of dark, spark-speckled smoke by the time he set out for school at nine.

In the school yard the older boys stood about in groups, their chestnut conker contests flaring alternately into breathy bursts of admiration and savage arguments. The younger ones, arms outstretched, raced between these groups, swooping and swerving, making a didgery-do whine, a nasal wail pitched to sound like a single engine plane. Others just stood around gormlessly, vacant observers of it all.

As Matt approached Carmody's room to collect the roll book he began to rehearse what he intended to say, planning to make it clear to Carmody that he knew he'd been duped into doing the translation and that he wouldn't be up for anything like it again. He anticipated that Carmody would pretend to be unaware of the nature of the broadcast, a position Matt figured he could use to his advantage. He gripped the door knob, dallied for a few seconds while he pieced together his opening lines. *If I'd known what was going on in Colls I wouldn't have gone near the place. Pro-German propaganda in Irish. Telling people how hard the going was in Russia …*

'Well, I hear you were the man of the match at the tennis on Saturday.' Carmody's voice boomed across the room before Matt had fully closed the door behind him.

Matt stalled.

'I don't know about that,' he smiled by way of response to the jocular way Carmody had spoken. 'I didn't make a complete fool of myself anyway.'

Carmody, Matt observed, was twitching and blinking as though he was in some way physically uncomfortable.

'I'd never played before,' Matt added.

'A skilful game, tennis.' He nodded as he spoke, stopping abruptly before he added, 'Not to everyone's liking, though.'

'Mrs Sheridan just asked me …'

'Ah no, no don't get me wrong. I have no particular objection to you playing the game, though I need hardly tell you that there are those who would.' His eyes narrowed, causing his whole face to tighten. The clamour of the pupils lining up outside the door grew louder.

Matt instantly grasped what he was getting at and was on the point of saying so when Carmody, in an impatient burst said, 'Surely you know that. Surely you know what people think of tennis.' His forehead crinkled. 'I mean tea-ching young boys, turning out decent Irishmen.' Matt felt his scalp tingle. He didn't need to be reminded that tennis was among those games identified by the Gaelic Athletic Association as 'foreign', and though its members, Matt and his brothers among them, were not officially banned from playing, as they were some other 'foreign' games, it was, Matt knew all too well, looked on as unpatriotic. But like his brothers and his friends, Matt regarded the prohibition as reactionary and divisive. He wanted to point this out to Carmody, wanted to tell him that things were moving on, but he held back, now keenly attuned to Carmody's tightly controlled vexation.

A yawp from the hall prompted Matt to reach for the roll book on the desk.

'It doesn't matter to me if I never play tennis again.' He spoke decisively, anxious not to get on the wrong side of Carmody.

'You can play all you like as far as I'm concerned, but it'll mean putting a stop to the training you're doing with the under-twelves. The boys'll be disappointed, but there is no question of using the pitch beyond, no question of using it, if tennis is your ...' He paused for a second or two, crinkled his nose, then in a bemused, sneering tone, said '... your fancy.'

'It was just a one-off thing to oblige Mrs Sheridan,' Matt said, swallowing the surge of anger he felt just looking at Carmody, his face bunched into an insinuating smirk, all the while trying to make out that there was some authority who would see to it that he was prohibited from training the under-twelves on the GAA pitch if he played 'foreign' games, when clearly that authority was Carmody himself.

'We can't have you running with the hare and hunting

with the hound,' Carmody laughed drily, creating a smoke screen, behind which he slipped in the phrase, 'better to stick with your own.'

The resolve Matt had mustered to tell him how he felt about the translating, now no more than a distant wish, was dealt a fatal blow when, still laughing, Carmody added, 'I hear you went back to Coll's the night after, offering to listen in.'

'No. I mean yes. I was just passing by. I'd made a hames of it the day before and I thought …' He drew breath, casting about for what to say next, then lapsed into an explanation for the poor job he'd made of the translation, 'I couldn't understand the accent. Donegal, I think it was. And the radio reception was terrible. The signal was gone altogether half the time …'

'Listen to that racket. You better get going before those hooligans have the place torn asunder.'

'Quiet,' Matt roared as soon as he stepped into the hall. '*Ciúnas, a dúirt mé.*' Jabbing the air with his index finger he pointed to the end of the line, ordering the three boys bunched at the front and blocking access to the classroom door to move.

The exchange with Carmody, forced to the back of his thoughts in the clattery moil of the classroom, flared up every now and then, sparking a flash of anger, rapidly eclipsed by a glut of demands.

'Sir, my father says he knows you and that you are a right good scholar.'

The boy was first in a line of fifth-class pupils queuing up beside Matt's desk, copybook in hand, ready to have his homework corrected. Matt registered and banished the boy's surname, Costigan, in the same instant.

'Is that so, Pádraig?' he said, his gaze roamed over the other class, which he'd directed to prepare for a mental arithmetic test. He looked down at the copybook and ticked the work mechanically.

'*Go maith, Pádraig.* Good. Very good.' He closed the copybook, held it out for the boy to take, determined not to acknowledge the connection.

As he corrected the next pupil's homework, he looked up again, allowing his rapid survey of the room to stall when he came to Éamon, Pádraig's younger brother. An image of their father sitting on the car seat in the dark corner of Coll's outhouse shot to the forefront of his thoughts, his demand to know if anything was said about 'here' now taking on a wider significance in the light of the impression he'd formed of the two boys over the previous week.

From the beginning he'd noted how focused, how keen they both were. He'd actively encouraged their enthusiasm, listened to what they had to say, even when, as happened in the very first history lesson on Monday afternoon, they more or less took the floor. Both hands had shot up at the mention of history and, like a well-practised operatic duet, they rattled off an account of the heroic part their grandfather had played in the War of Independence some twenty years previously. Neither that war nor any of the events leading to it were on the syllabus, but Matt nonetheless let them go on, hoping to use some aspect of the account they were spouting to introduce the lesson he'd prepared on the Vikings. That opportunity did not arise, at least not until they had given a blow-by-blow description of their grandfather's arrest by the Black and Tans, which included the thoughts that had gone through his head 'when a gun was pressed against his eye', followed by a detailed account of his daredevil escape. This was capped by an image of him as one of a fearless band of warriors rampaging through centuries of Irish history, asserting the nation's claim to sovereignty. This group included distant, mythical warriors such as Cú Chulainn as well as the eleventh-century High King, Brian Boru. Astonished at the performance but at the same time increasingly anxious to intervene, Matt seized on the name Brian Boru, quickly pointing out that he was the man who in 1014, had brought about the defeat of the Vikings in the Battle of Clontarf. Once he had made the connection, he began to work his way through the lesson he'd prepared on the Vikings, satisfied that the wide birth he'd given the Costigans would ensure that they stayed quiet for the rest of the lesson. Both, however, remained on high alert, hands up, mouths open waiting for the moment when they could resume. Matt tried to ignore them, expecting that they'd tire of waiting and slump, with most of the others, into sleepy, mid-afternoon passivity. Not so: they grew more eager. Pádraig, now half-standing with his arm extending over the head of the boy in front of him, virtually begged for a chance to speak.

'*A Mháistir, a Mháistir,*' Pádraig pleaded every time Matt stopped to draw breath, steadily eroding his resolve to continue.

'Well, Pádraig?' Matt eventually said.

'My grandda …' And so it all began again, amended at the outset to include most of what Matt had said about the Vikings, but soon lapsing into the same list of thoughts that ran through his grandfather's mind when the Black and Tans pressed a gun to his eye, the same step-by-step account of his escape. His brother Éamon had less to say this time around. He just waited, pouncing like a prowling leopard whenever Pádraig made the slightest slip in what Matt now saw was a view of the past written in stone.

'I have this lad by the name of Costigan …' Matt said to Canning as they left the school that afternoon. 'Never shuts up, he …'

'Say no more.' Canning raised his hand as though to defend himself against what he knew was to follow. 'Didn't I have him for two years? Him and his grandfather.'

Matt laughed.

'The grandfather was the longest-serving councillor in the county. No job was to be had, except through him. *Costigan or the boat to England.* That's the way it was put. The son Murt is a supervisor on the roads, but to listen to him you'd think he was the minister, with the way he throws his weight about.'

When, at breaktime, Canning called to collect Matt on his way to Carmody's room, as he had done every day so far, his shorn bullet head popping through the narrowly opened door Matt told him to go ahead, explaining that he had a few things to do. He could not, he felt, rely on himself to overlook what had passed between him and Carmody.

Sitting there, mulling over that exchange, his thoughts drifted to Murt Costigan and on to Éamon and Pádraig, thoughts that in a meandering way led him to wonder if Murt, was driven by some deep-seated desire to earn a place, as his father seemingly had, among those who, in the Costigans' eyes, had brought glory to Ireland. Matt wondered if Costigan had approached Carmody directly or if there was an intermediary, thoughts that once again evoked his over enthusiastic reading of 'Tír na nÓg' in the classroom.

It remained clammy all day, the sense of an approaching storm hanging heavily by mid afternoon. At the end of school, as the last line of pupils had just tailed out of the classroom and was beginning to break up in the hall, Matt walked across to close the windows. As he forced the first one down, he was suddenly paralyzed by the sight of Madelene in her peppermint-coloured muslin frock, leaning against the wall outside the school, her back to him.

Dixie must have told her I called yesterday, he thought, straining like a trapped colt to bolt out, but reined back by the knowledge that just speaking to her with the pupils about, would, in the ever watchful eyes of Rathisland, soon become a talking point and, before long, a scandal. Nonetheless he was hell-bent on making a move. The two older classes, taught by Carmody, finished some twenty minutes later. He'd have to strike before then. Meanwhile, he had little choice but to wait in the classroom until his own pupils, still skulking about outside, had gone.

In between forays to the window to monitor the pace at which the coast was clearing, he began to prepare what he'd say to her. Something about *Gone with the Wind*, he figured, something that might recreate the opportunity he had so carelessly squandered in the cornfield. And so it was, about ten minutes later, he stood, no more than a dozen paces away from her and yelled, 'Better look out, there's a Yankie army marching this direction, 'bout to burn the town down!'

The person who suddenly swung around, a pale woman in her early thirties, was clearly frightened. She looked about, saw no one and glared fearfully at him as he approached. He stood before her, speechless for a moment or two before he mumbled, 'Sorry, I thought you were someone else.'

Chapter 8

On the way to Colls' the following evening, Matt was seized by a notion than Madelene was different from how he imagined her. In trying to imagine that difference, he failed to imagine her at all. So when he spotted her coming out of the house, she seemed like an impostor, less and yet more real than the Madelene who'd occupied his every thought.

She looked at him impassively as he approached.

'Oh, hello,' words she inflected to sound like a question. Not a trace of the lilting *well I do dee-clare* with which she'd greeted him in the cornfield the previous Friday.

'They're already in there.' She raised her hand, directing Matt to the outhouse, adding, before he had a chance to tell her he hadn't come to seek out Costigan and Dixie that her aunts were 'very bothered about it'. And with that, she turned to walk across to where Statia and Rose were seated in two faded green basket chairs, their hands cupped on their foreheads to guard against the low autumn sunlight filtering through the great sycamore at the other side of the yard. Matt looked across at them. Smiled, raised his hand a little. They nodded, each in the same slow way, like presiding matrons from a bygone era, capable of conveying a whole range of sentiments in a short, slight bow. Among those sentiments was unease, or so Matt felt. They think I'm part of this. They think I'm here as some kind of sidekick to Costigan, fears he instantly rushed into words.

'Look. I haven't anything to do with what's going on in there,' he called out after Madelene, 'I was tricked into coming here on Friday.' She slowed down but quickly began to gather pace again.

'The reason why I'm here now is to tell them …' he raised his voice, '… tell your man Costigan, it would have to be reported to the gardaí,' a lie into which he stumbled in a reckless attempt to place himself on her side. He went to follow her but changed course abruptly and stomped over to the outhouse, now certain that Madelene and her aunts believed he and Costigan were involved in a shady political escapade and were putting Dixie at risk. There was nothing for it except to confront Costigan head-on; that way they'd soon see where he stood.

*

Dixie, leaning over the wireless in the half-light, looked up when Matt appeared in the doorway, then glanced swiftly at Costigan sitting at the edge of the car seat, all his attention directed to the broadcast. He raised his chin a little, his mouth slackening to form a gaping expression that fell somewhere between recognition and welcome. The national anthem, the signature music, was still playing.

Best to let it run for a bit, Matt thought. Have something definite with which to challenge him.

The scratchy recording of 'A Tiny Sprig of Shamrock', following the national anthem, was accompanied by vigorous foot-tapping from Costigan. This accompaniment ended abruptly when a high, whistling sound, punctuated by what appeared to Matt to be Morse code, drowned out the tune. Just as Dixie touched the dial to relocate the station, the word *'fáilte'* sounded. The English language broadcast that followed marked the anniversary of an atrocity carried out by British forces during the War of Independence in Balbriggan: Balbriggan of all places. Matt could scarcely believe it. He took it as a sign that fate was on his side. He wanted to announce there and then that he was from Ballbriggan, that he knew everything there was to know about the place, but had never heard of any of the events to which the presenter was referring. All made up. Barefaced, anti-British propaganda. Hoping that there was more to come, more fabricated material with which to support his challenge, he held back. And so there was. Lots of it. All mounting steadily, as the presenter went on to claim that English military cadets, aided by the Royal Irish Constabulary and the Black and Tans had broken into the home of a shop owner, whose name Matt didn't catch. This man was brutally beaten and dragged to the local barracks. On the way he saw two young men lying in the gutter, bayoneted to death. Twenty-five houses in the town were set alight, forcing the people to flee to the countryside where they hid in ditches and drains until their persecutors had left. All this was purported to have happened a little over two decades previously.

'Not a word of that's true,' Matt said bluntly the instant it ended.

'If your opinion is wanted, it'll be asked for,' Costigan

said in a slow, emphatic way. Dixie sniggered nervously.

'It's a pack of lies. Unadulterated, anti-British propaganda.'

'No one's asking you to listen to it.' Costigan nodded in the direction of the door. Then signalled to Dixie to turn up the radio. Matt moved forward until he was as close to Costigan as the clutter of the outhouse allowed. The oily, ferric smell gave way to a stale, mealy whiff.

'I'll go alright, but I may as well tell you where I'm going.' He leant down towards Costigan, expecting him to ask where, ready to say 'the garda barracks'. But Costigan just stared at him, his expression questioning in a vaguely fearful way.

'I'm going to the barracks before they get wind of this and ...'

'You can go all you fucken well like,' Costigan cut in, snapping back the authority he'd conceded to Matt '... but just remember there's no law against listening to a wireless.' He gestured towards Dixie, who was crouched down, trying to hide behind it. Matt spun around to face him, accidentally kicking over an empty drum.

'You know where this could get you?'

Dixie crouched down further, twisting as though trying to make himself smaller, more compact.

'These people ...' Matt swung back to face Costigan, then pointed in the direction of the house. 'These people don't want this going on here.'

'Who the fuck are you to say what they want or don't want?'

'I'm not ...' he hesitated, 'I was codded into coming here to do the Irish on Friday. And if it's found out, and I'm telling you it will be, I'm ...' He leaned forward, pointed forcibly at himself, 'It's me who they'll start watching.'

Costigan was about to respond when Matt, jabbing his

index finger at the wireless, said, 'You know just as well as I do that Carmody kept away from this for fear it would land him in the Curragh. And mean his job. And I can tell you this for nothing, it's not going to mean my job.'

Costigan's lips curled at the edge. 'It could mean unity for Ireland, if you weren't all so fucken concerned with your jobs.' He glared at Dixie, a threatening demand for support, but Dixie had all but disappeared behind the wireless. The signal, crisply clear until then, became a fuzzy tangle of foreign voices. Costigan gestured impatiently to Dixie to relocate it. When Dixie didn't budge he leapt up, shoved Dixie out of the way and reached for the tuning knob. The garbled voices disappeared altogether, leaving only a loud hiss. 'This isn't the only short wave in Rathisland.' He glared defiantly at Matt, as though to impress on him that he oughtn't consider he had put the kibosh on things.

He then turned to Dixie, 'You can take your wireless and shove it up your arse, you ungrateful little cunt. And don't come looking to me when you want batteries.' He pointed impatiently at the wireless. 'You've seen the last battery, wet or dry, you're going to see for many's the long day.' He stormed out, leaving the outhouse door open.

Matt exhaled, allowing his arms to fall loosely to either side. It was, he felt, as good an outcome, better, much better than he could have expected.

Dixie, like a boy checking the lie of the land from the safety of his hiding place, peeked over the top of the wireless.

'He was supplying you with batteries?' Matt spoke quietly.

Dixie didn't answer.

Out in the yard, Matt made his way over to Madelene and her aunts, breathing in the fresh, dusky air.

You needn't be concerned, I've seen to that, Costigan won't be coming back. He half-whispered to himself by way of rehearsal.

'You needn't be concerned …' he began in a raised voice from the middle of the yard, throwing his head back and smiling in a bid to underplay his success, but obliged to look over his shoulder when he saw that Madelene's and her aunts' attention was focused not on him but on Dixie. Determined to reveal his part in getting Costigan to leave, Matt picked up pace, speaking rapidly as he went.

'All that had to be done was to have the danger of it pointed out. It was just …' He shrugged as though to shake off, in advance, the credit he believed they were going to heap on him. And they were pleased, pleased in a coiling, cat-like way, though they were not, it soon became apparent, going to say so. Madelene, on the other hand, smiled openly at him, visibly delighted.

'Danger?' Rose sat up in her chair. 'Danger?' She placed her open hand on her breastbone, spreading her fingers as if to search for the extent of a wound.

'Yes,' Matt said authoritatively, poised to continue, when Dixie sidled up to them.

The contented way in which Rose and Statia smiled at Dixie and, more importantly, Madelene's soft, sympathetic expression as she too looked at him, established Dixie as an intermediary through which Matt felt obliged to act in order to reach them.

'What I said inside …' Matt cast his eyes in the direction

of the outhouse, 'was, I mean, I wasn't going to be going to the gardaí. Not really. No.'

Dixie fixed his gaze on the ground.

'Where's the programme coming from? Who's putting it out?' Matt asked as amicably as he could, a question he hoped would steer the conversation to a point where the full significance of Costigan's departure would become apparent to Madelene.

'Berlin,' Dixie said with unexpected confidence.

'Hardly from Berlin in Irish?'

'Oh no, it's from Berlin. That's for definite.' The plethora of technical details about signals, transmitters and sources of interference with which Dixie supported this claim, his head down throughout, led Matt to suppose that he knew what he was talking about. When, in an almost incoherent rush, he then began to explain, providing another jumble of technical data, why the broadcasts could not be coming from a local transmitter, Matt became even more convinced. But he had to wait until a gap appeared in this unstoppable burst, facts splattering here, there and everywhere as though released by a series of tightly coiled springs, before he could voice the question he'd been itching to ask.

'And that's what your man Costigan was interested in. He wanted to tune into the Germans?'

The answer, Matt anticipated, would make it clear that Costigan was there as a would-be champion of German war aims. Dixie looked up for the first time, his blank expression implying that he hadn't heard the question properly, or somehow didn't understand it.

'That's what Costigan wanted?' Matt spoke slowly, adding, even more slowly, 'He wanted to listen to what was coming from Berlin, to see if they had plans for here?'

Dixie continued to look blankly at Matt, who, confused

by his carry-on, looked to Madelene, then to Rose and Statia appealing for an explanation. It was an appeal that found no quarter with Rose or Statia, but triggered a flicker of sympathy, short-lived though nonetheless discernable, in Madelene. Enough to make him persevere.

'He wanted to hear if the Germans were coming?'

'Yes.' Dixie's gaze shot downwards again. Then, like a sullen schoolboy giving way under interrogation, reluctantly added, 'There was nothing about it. Nothing any night about them coming here. Bar in the Irish, he thought.'

'Costigan was taking a hell of a chance, coming here.' He smiled at the others in a bid to assure them there was no criticism of Dixie implied. Then waited, sure, now that he'd got Dixie to admit to what was going on, that they would acknowledge what he'd achieved in getting rid of Costigan. And while he waited he began to anticipate the impact that acknowledgment would have on Madelene, certain that within seconds she would be smiling admiringly at him.

'There's a bit of a chill in the evenings.' Statia gripped both sides of her cardigan and, shuddering a little, drew them together. Rose responded by stirring this way and that in her chair, a bird ruffling its plumage to occupy as much of its nest as possible. Both stood up in unison, lifted the flattened cushions off their chairs, held them up and began to shake them. Dixie, realizing he was free to go, sloped off in the direction of the derelict glass house.

'No. Let me.' Matt rushed over to take the chair that Madelene was lifting.

'You can take that one.' She crooked her elbow and directed it to the other chair, an invitation that reached Matt as though electrically charged, impelling him to dive at the chair, swing it way up into the air over his head, ready, like a primitive warrior brandishing a heavy weapon, to do whatever was required of him.

Statia and Rose trekked into the house, each carrying a puffed-up cushion in a ceremonial sort of way, holding them out in front like courtiers about to present a precious object to a royal personage. Matt followed with the basket chair, swinging it down as he approached the door. Best to turn and back in, he figured, exaggerating the care necessary, easing the chair onto the step, blocking Madelene's progress while he leaned this way and that, estimating the space available on both sides.

'I was really just going for a walk out this way when I decided to come down. I'm still going on it. I mean I'm going to go on, if you wanted to come.' Only then did he look up from the elaborate measuring performance he was staging.

Madelene went to say something, *Yes*, Matt thought, but checked herself and, in a peculiarly prissy voice said, 'I'll have to ask,' to which Matt instantly replied, 'Of course.'

'Into the right. The parlour. Just leave it anywhere in there. Thanks.'

Madelene followed him, plonked her chair just inside the door. But then, instead of going down the hall to ask her aunts if she could go for a walk, as Matt anticipated, she just flurried upstairs. He rested his hand on the hall stand, quickly removing it when he discovered how unsteady it was. A few steps away, on top of a narrow lacquered table was a dusty glass dome, home to a snarling, stuffed otter with a waxy fish gripped between its teeth. Matt moved closer, went down on his hunkers to examine it, fascinated by the taxidermist's attention to detail. There were even tufts of heather or gorse in between the otter's finely paired, hook-like toenails, the whole display mysteriously complimented by the smell of freshly cut wood and sweetened by what seemed like the scent of marzipan or toasting almonds.

His thoughts turned back to Dixie, then to the much discussed German invasion, recalling debates about it at dinner time in the training college refectory. Every one had an opinion. So much so that the conversations, particularly when there was a big development like the American entry, grew thunderously loud, with anything up to a half-dozen fellows, competing at any one of the many tables, to have their say. Some argued that the government should invite the Germans to come, that it would do away with the border and so create a United Ireland. Others, including Matt, baulked at this idea, insisting that the best stance was the one taken, neutrality. Whatever the opinion, pro- or anti-German, the Third Reich was much admired. It was audacious, highly energized, decisive. The whole thing exuded a vibrancy, a sense of possibility. Matt sometimes imagined a gleaming Wehrmacht platoon marching out towards the college from the city centre, the deep timbre of their singing filling the sky as they approached Drumcondra Bridge. He imagined them commandeering the college. There was beer, long trestle tables laden down with large, frothing jugs of it. And a gymnastics display in the grounds, staged by hundreds of limby Frauleins; leaping legends of the opening ceremony of the 1936 Olympics. It felt like a liberation: not so much a liberation from the old familiar oppressor, Britain, as from caution, or fear, or whatever it was that kept things the way they were.

When, eventually, Madelene reappeared, she had changed into a different outfit: a voluminously skirted, satiny looking frock, printed with large orange daisies; a navy-blue cardigan slung over her shoulders. She headed directly out the door, skipped down the steps as if on her way to a party.

'Don't you have to ask if you can go?'

'Oh yes.' She laughed.

'I'm going for a walk,' she called back, surprising Matt when she didn't wait for a reply, making him wonder why she'd told him she'd have to ask in the first place.

They crossed the yard quickly. The whispery rustle of Madelene's frock filled the space around them, creating an air of collusion, accentuating Matt's sense of stealing away into the night, a feeling he was trying to find a nonchalant way of expressing, when Madelene spoke: 'I didn't twig all that about the Germans coming.' She glanced back at the house.

'No one can tell what's going to happen, though with the way Russia is going it's less likely they'll come now. Anyway, it's all a long way from here, nothing to get too worked-up about, at least not on a lovely night like this.' He smiled and remained smiling as Madelene asked how he knew so much about it.

'I don't really. And even less since I came here, with fuzzy BBC.' Matt closed his eyes and inhaled deeply, reiterating how lovely a night it was.

'Sounds to me like you do.' She spoke with a mix of admiration and rebuke.

'Well, maybe.' He shrugged. 'We talked a lot about it in the college, but it was all just that; talk.' He looked up at the darkening sky, allowing his gaze to drift slowly to the last of the day's light spindling out from the faraway horizon.

'Dad's stationed in Scotland, right up at the top. Looking out for ships from Norway.'

Matt was slow to respond: 'And you were evacuated from London?'

Madelene laughed, 'I never thought of it that way.' She continued to laugh.

'What's so funny?'

'Oh, nothing. Just seeing myself arriving here with one

of those tags with my name on it. You know, one of those big evacuee tags?' She swung around and with the index fingers of both hands, marked out the shape of an evacuee tag on the front of her frock, then pirouetted as though to model it. Matt's laughter resonated in the crisp evening air, encircling them, tightening them into the same moment, causing him to feel oddly removed from himself, elevated onto an altogether new plane of experience.

'It was great that you came on the walk. Great, really. I mean that. I didn't know if you would. I called down the other evening. I wanted to tell you it was me singing, that it was me you heard through the open window. I don't know why I said it wasn't. Probably 'cos I can't sing. I just about got through the test for singing that you have to do to get into the college.' He wanted to stop talking but he couldn't. 'There were some really good singers in my year. There was one fellow, Austin Maher, who could have gone professional if he wanted to. I wouldn't be surprised if he does. I mean he's the same age as me, twenty-one, which is young for a singer.' Matt began to hear himself speak as though from a distance away, his words rebounding, charged with an energy that bore no relation to what he was saying. 'If I was him I would give it a go. Enter the Feis Cheoil, that way he'd be ...' Matt moved close, then closer still, suddenly silenced by the brush of Madelene's frock against his thigh. She skipped ahead.

'Dad says I'm better off here. Safer. I used to love coming. Every summer. I couldn't wait. Aunty Rose and Statia ...' Her voice trailed off, gathering pace again when she asked, 'What did that man have to do with the Germans coming?'

'Costigan?'

'Yes,' she said eagerly, 'Costigan.'

'Costigan is a fool.' Matt paused to rein in his exasperation, then continued in a calmer voice, 'He was hoping, still is I'd say, to hear about their invasion plans. He was supplying Dixie with batteries, which can't be got for love nor money and Dixie was getting him the station he wanted. Stupid thinking it would be announced on the radio like that. Even if it was going to happen. Anyway, you were saying, a minute ago, about coming here for the summers, about how much you liked it.' Matt edged up closer, tensing while he waited to see if she was going to skip ahead again. She did, but not straight away.

'See. You do know all about it.' She drew breath, creating the expectation that she was about to continue, which she didn't. It struck Matt that he ought to have agreed that he knew a lot about it, that he had at least as good a grasp of what was happening as the next man.

'I only came in the first place because Carmody asked me to translate something from Irish. Bits of the programmes were in Irish. He didn't say what it was.' He looked directly at her, continuing to do so by walking sideways. 'You saw, on Friday I had the dictionary. You thought it was a bible.'

'I only said that,' Madelene laughed, 'but you have to admit it looked like one.'

'Listen, listen to that.' Matt's voice brimmed with amazement. He angled his head sharply, drawing attention to the way the swish of her dress and the click of the steel heel tips on his boots combined to form a rhythmic sound. 'It's like the start of a jazz solo, you know, kettle drum and brushed cymbals.' He beat an imaginary drum with his large open hands. 'Like this, bmm, tish, bmm, tish …'

Madelene looked at him, her expression a mix of bemusement and curiosity.

'Rules out being a robber. Steel tips.' Matt laughed. Stupid, he immediately thought. Stupid, saying that.

'What would happen if the gardaí found out?'

Unsteadied by the way the conversation kept swinging back to Costigan and Dixie, and trying all the while to control a near-overwhelming urge to declare his hand, he did not, he could not, reply. He was convinced that if he as much as opened his mouth, those raw, artless words he was holding back would stampede forward and force their way out.

'Probably nothing,' he then heard himself say, in what sounded, though did not feel like, his everyday voice. He paused briefly to steady himself. 'They'd keep an eye on the place, Costigan too. But anyone they think would help the Germans, the IRA, or what's left of them, is already behind bars. Interned in the Curragh.'

'Oh.' Madelene raised her hands, ran her fingers through her hair on both sides of her head, then flicked it back. 'That's awful.'

'How? How do you mean awful?'

'Prison. Being put in a prison. I'd hate to be in prison.' She shuddered.

'But they're … they could cause the whole country to be bombed. Bringing the Germans here.' He waved his hand across the quiet, loamy fields to the left, a gauze of mist imperceptibly settling on them as evening gave way to night. 'People killed, right, left and centre, like in Poland.'

'Two Polish girls came to my school just after it all started.'

'Tell me,' he looked directly at her. 'What do you … I mean what's there to do in Rathisland?'

'Well, there's, there's …' She hesitated, about, it seemed, to launch into a list of things when she said, 'nothing really.'

'I see that the cinema has shows on Wednesdays, Fridays and Sundays. *Show Boat* is on this week.'

'Yes. We went on Wednesday, though I'd seen it before, ages ago.'

The word *we* struck like a mallet. She means her aunts

he instantly assured himself, but still felt compelled to find out for certain. 'I'd say Rose and Statia liked it.'

'They said they wanted to go, but I think it was because I said I wouldn't mind going again. They're always thinking of things we can do.'

'Out to spoil you.' Matt chuckled, swung his arm around her shoulder, squeezed it firmly, let go before it became too significant.

'Hardly anything has come that I haven't seen before.' She pulled the rim of her cardigan up towards her chin.

'If it was Dublin. You see, Dublin is different. Totally different. I mean if I was teaching there, I could go all I liked, but it isn't the same here. I could probably go, but I think it would have to be something, something everyone was going to, like that one about all the nuns escaping from wherever it was.'

'That's all you can go to?'

Matt wondered if she understood what he was trying to tell her. But then, as though prompted by a different self suddenly come to life, he found himself asking how in God's name she could be expected to understand why a grown man might not be free to go to the cinema whenever he wanted. It was, he told himself, his own fault, trying to explain something that was, in the first place, absurd. In this way, Madelene's incomprehension, until then a difficulty in grasping the facts, now appeared as an uncanny ability to see things for what they were, to see right through those layers of caution in which Rathisland was shrouded. He was engulfed by a new swell of affection for her. He put his arm around her shoulder again, leaving it there a little longer, sensing he might levitate when she did not resist for what was no more than a moment or two, but felt like an eternity.

The evening was closing in. It would soon be time to turn back. Matt could feel the opportunity to make an arrangement to see her again slipping away, feel it almost as if it were an animate thing, going cold, dying.

'I'm going to see, I'm cycling out to see Cloneeshel Abbey. On Saturday, if you'd like to come? I mean we could go somewhere else. There's lots of places.'

'That'd be nice,' she began speculatively, 'but I don't know if I can, if I'll still be here.' Her eyes blinked as she spoke, a nervousness in her movements that stopped Matt from asking, straight out, what she meant.

'It's just that I've asked Dad if I can go back, if I can start nursing. I've asked him before and he said that once the war is over, that it won't last.'

'But it's not over, or nearly over.'

She nodded slowly, a gesture that confused Matt, leading him to say the first thing that came into his mind. 'And what does your mother think?'

'Mum isn't at home at the moment. That's why Dad doesn't want me being in the house on my own. Which I won't be if I start nursing.' She turned to Matt and in an insistent, almost indignant voice, told him that the course in Bristol General, where she'd got a place over a year ago, was fully residential.

Afraid that it was all whittling away to nothing, that he would arrive back in the yard without any arrangement to see her again, or worse, that she was working her way to saying no, he leapt ahead.

'I'll tell you what. I'll cycle by the top of the lane at ten on Saturday. If you're there you're there and if you're not, you're not.' He turned towards her, looked directly at her. She averted her head, then slowed down as she pored over the mechanics of the plan. 'Yes,' she said, lingering on the word. This she followed through with another 'Yes', fuller, less equivocal, more hopeful, Matt felt. He splayed his fingers, about to sling his arm over her shoulder again, but instantly bunched them together, determined to leave well enough alone.

He didn't know where Cloneeshel Abbey was, how far away, how big or small, interesting or uninteresting. He could not, at first, remember how or where he'd heard of it. Only when it struck him that it mightn't exist at all did he recall that it was one of a number of places in the locality which Mrs Sheridan had rattled off as 'worth a visit'. Somehow the name had lodged in his mind and, uprooted by desperation, came bounding forward the instant he began to search for somewhere to bring Madelene, somewhere other than the cinema.

Darkness had fully fallen by the time the house came into view. Its dormer windows, quivering beacons of amber candlelight, took on a firmer shape, their light sharpening to an incandescent yellow as Matt and Madelene made their way down the lane.

*

In the low-ceilinged, apple-smelling kitchen Rose and Statia waited for Madelene's return in fretful silence. By this stage the room was alive with long-ago conversations. Fraught conversations; rows and recriminations; their father roaring at their brother Larry, his thunderous voice shaking the house to its foundations; scenes Rose and Statia did not, on any account, want to revisit. But their concern for Madelene, rooted, as it was, in that past, forced them to look back. And so they found themselves swept into a story that had begun two decades previously with the hiring of a new kitchen maid, eighteen-year-old Mary Teehan, mother to a baby daughter, Madelene, within the year.

Another chapter of that story was, to Rose and Statia's way of thinking, already in progress when Madelene skipped down the front steps in her satiny dress and out into the darkening evening with Matt. Too afraid to ask each other if she might have the same reckless impulses as her mother, too afraid to have their worst fears confirmed, they did not speak. They pottered about in the kitchen, moving things this way and that, more convinced by the minute that Madelene had set out on a path that sooner or later, would lead, not just to her own ruin, but to theirs as well. By the time she arrived back they had all but witnessed the last stage in the demise of the Colls, a process begun by Madelene's mother, *that Jezebel* as they'd so often referred to her, who'd come among them, a serpent in their Eden.

Chapter 9

'What if you or me wanted to take up with a girl, I mean. What would be the run of it?'

Canning, who'd agreed to meet Matt on Wednesday evening in the Commercial Hotel, Dowlings, looked quizzically at him.

'It would depend.'

'On what?'

'On the circumstance. Who she was and what way you went about it.'

'That's what I'm asking. How to go about it, I mean in a way that wouldn't be against how people, Father Finn, Mr Carmody and you know, how they wouldn't think badly of it.'

Canning looked from side to side, making sure, which he'd done every few minutes since they'd arrived, that there was no one within earshot. His smile narrowed to a grin when, like a priest in the confessional, he tilted his head towards Matt.

'Who is she?'

'No. I'm only just saying, if …'

'Do you think I came down in the last shower?' Canning laughed. 'There isn't a person in the town or three miles within it who doesn't know you were seen out on the Castle Wall Road with Madelene Coll.' He pursed his lips and nodded, conspicuously satisfied to have outwitted Matt. Although well aware that surveillance of everyone by everyone else was the order of the day in Rathisland, Matt was still taken aback. Maybe someone in the cluster of cottages just beyond the lane spotted them, or maybe someone herding cattle in the fields, thoughts that undermined his sense of having been alone with Madelene, making their walk seem just part of everything else that went on.

When, a few days beforehand, he and Canning had arranged to meet for the drink, Canning had outlined the procedure like an intelligence officer instructing a new recruit.

'It'll have to be the hotel,' he'd begun, reminding Matt, though he did not need to be reminded, that they could not go to any of the many other pubs in the town. Canning then went on to explain that as teachers they had positions to uphold and could not be rubbing shoulders with the very people for whom they were upholding these positions in the first place. 'It was,' he said, 'a question of having people's respect.' He'd muttered something about 'loose talk' and 'how a fellow could loose the run of himself with a drink', nodding knowingly to indicate that there was a long litany of other, similarly well founded reasons why it would have to be Dowlings. They could not, he'd warned, enter through the bar door. They'd have to knock on the front door, the residents' entrance. Mrs Dowling, he'd assured Matt, would answer it and show them into the Commercial Room, where they could expect to find 'a few commercial travellers having a quiet drink'.

And so it was that they were shown into that room by Mrs Dowling, where, as Canning had predicted, there were a few commercial travellers having a quiet drink, two of them chatting, one reading a newspaper and another working on his accounts. The room, half-public, half-private, had something of the atmosphere of a speakeasy about it: cigarette smoke, hushed voices, an unspoken acknowledgment of illicitness.

'I don't want it to go against me. Asking her out, if you know what I mean?' Matt looked anxiously at Canning, willing him to respond sympathetically.

'I know what you mean alright, but I'd have to be honest with you and say it might.'

Canning lifted his glass, sipped the lemony looking ale through his bunched lips, all the while observing Matt.

'In what way?'

'Well, in the way that it would be different if you were a few years older and people saw it as leading to the altar, but the way it is, what I'm trying to say, is that it might, seeing what age you are, be looked on as a bit on the gamey side, if you know what I mean? Her being no more than eighteen or nineteen.'

Matt felt his face redden. He lifted his glass, held it tilted in front of his throbbing face, then slowly sipped the rim.

'And what with her being English and all.' Canning opened his mouth a little, threw his head back then slowly brought it forward, a firm, insinuating nod that cut Matt to the quick. In a bid for time to compose himself, Matt asked Canning what he meant.

'It's not what I mean. It's the way people think. You know just as well as I do that they'd be inclined to see an English lassie as a bit freer with herself. That that's what you were after.'

Matt didn't answer.

'I'm not saying that you are. It's just the way people might be inclined to look at it.'

Overcome by a sense of powerlessness, a low, sinking feeling that he wouldn't ever be free to steer things in the direction in which he wanted to, Matt lifted his glass, wondering, as he drank, if Rathisland would always be watching, always be waiting for the moment he stepped out of line, always be there eager to pass sentence.

'God, it's like living in fucken occupied territory.'

Canning's hee-haw laugh prompted one of the commercial travellers to look up from his paperwork. Canning froze, then shrank apologetically into his chair.

'The only difference is that you can't rightly tell who the occupiers are.'

Canning just remained exactly as he was, head down, shoulders slightly hunched, expression solemn.

'The same again?' Matt pointed to Canning's half-empty glass and before he could answer, went in search of Mrs Dowling.

'Do you think …' he began as he slumped back into his chair, '… you'll spend the rest of your life here?'

Canning lifted his half-empty glass and to Matt's amazement swallowed it in a single, uninterrupted swig.

'Who know what they'll be doing for the rest of their lives?' A smell of cooking, a ham boiling, Matt figured, wafted through the cigarette smoke when Mrs Dowling came with the drinks.

'I suppose.' Matt sat forward as she eased his glass onto the table. He watched the ale froth slide down the side of his glass, increasingly aware that Canning was staring at him. When he looked up, Canning continued to stare, his face fixed in a half-enquiring, half-fearful expression.

'I was wondering if I could ask a favour.'

'Fire ahead.'

'It's about what you were saying, if I was going to spend the rest of my life in Rathisland.' Canning took a worn, folded piece of what appeared to be copybook paper from his pocket.

'The only other person I've show this to is the mother.' He held it between his thumb and his forefinger, raising it up and down by flicking his wrist rhythmically. 'It's just some questions that I've to answer. No, not answer. Consider.'

Matt reached out to take the piece of paper but Canning didn't release it.

'I've put them to myself nearly every day for the past year or so and although I've answered them I can't tell where the answers are coming from, if you know what I mean.' He blinked a few times, a vulnerability about him now that made Matt uncomfortable.

'Here, give it to me.'

'I thought if I got someone to ask me them. The way it is I couldn't ask my mother because, well, you'll see.' He handed Matt the folded paper, picked up his glass and swilled almost the same amount as he had the last time.

'The first one is the one that I don't know the answer to. But, then sometimes I think I do.' Matt surveyed the questions, twelve in all, scripted in copperplate handwriting on the frayed centre page of a school copybook.

'I wrote to this priest in Kildare that I got the name of.'

Matt continued to read.

'He's well known for the advice he gives on vocations, but he doesn't see people, I mean he doesn't talk to them. Just writes.'

'What do you want me to do?' Matt, trying to conceal his incredulity, spoke from behind his tilted glass. 'Do you want me to ask them to you?'

Canning nodded vigorously, then leaned forward as though getting on his marks for a race.

'We'll start with the first, the one you're having the trouble with. "*Has God spoken to you?*" '

'The thing is I think He has, but how can I be sure?' Canning's eyes darted from side to side as he spoke. 'See, when I think too much about it I start thinking He hasn't and that's …' he ran the palm of his hand over his head, so agitated that Matt intervened: 'The way it works, as far as I understand it, is that if you think He spoke to you then He did.'

Canning was visibly relieved. 'That's it. That's exactly what Father Cullen said when I wrote asking him. It's a question of faith, he said. And that it was an insult to God to go looking for proof.' Canning reached for his glass and downed most of what was left.

'If you ask me, the real tricky ones come at the end.' Hoping to avoid asking the other questions, Matt jumped to number eleven. 'Do you …'

'No. No, definitely that one, the one about God speaking. That's the trickiest.' Canning's whole face was taut with conviction.

'Listen to me. Here's number eleven. Do you ever have bad thoughts?' Matt laughed.

'That's not the question.' Canning snapped.

'Alright.' Matt placed the page at arm's length and, affecting the mien of an examining magistrate, read the question in full. 'Do you ever have bad thoughts concerning women?'

'No.' Canning said firmly, casting his eyes downwards as he spoke.

Matt felt an immediate urge to laugh, to accuse Canning of being a liar, but Canning's unyielding expression, the immediacy with which he'd said no, the absence of any follow-on, jokey or otherwise, made him hold back. It struck him, very briefly, that he himself could be the abnormal one, that not everyone, maybe only a small few, were as plagued as he was by 'bad thoughts'.

'Well in that case you're home and dry, because if you can say no to that one, you don't have to answer the last one at all.' Matt looked around the room, then read out the question in a low, solemn voice. 'Do you actively entertain or actively resist these thoughts?'

Matt folded the page and held it out, anticipating, as Canning reluctantly took it, that it would end at that. But it didn't. Canning kept returning to it, each time demanding to know what Matt thought, quick to argue the toss when Matt assured him he had a vocation, but equally quick when Matt expressed doubt.

After the fourth round, Canning, now more tormented than ever, started to accuse Matt of trying to persuade him to become a priest against his will. Time to wind things up, Matt figured. But some twenty minutes later, outside the hotel in the cool, night air, just as they were about to part, Canning, in a meek, half-hearted way, said; 'Would you mind asking them again?'

'It's too dark. Some other time.' Matt strode ahead, keeping a pace or two in front of Canning all the way down Main Street.

*

On the Friday afternoon, the day before he was due to go to Cloneeshel Abbey with Madelene, the two classes, restless as they always were in the afternoons, suddenly bolted up out of their seats and, like a squadron about to be inspected, stood fiercely to attention. Matt swung around to find Father Finn standing in the doorway, his hand moving as though he was bouncing an invisible ball, bidding them to sit down. The linty scent of his hair oil wafted across the classroom mingling with a clammy, canvas shoe odour and the low-lying, blocked-drain smell. He remained in the doorway, a book in his outstretched hand.

'Don't let me disturb the good work.' He half-whispered, 'The play. Auditions on Monday. In the parochial house. Seven o' clock.' And with that he slipped out, will o' the wisp-like. Matt watched him disappear up the hall, wondering as he saw him tiptoeing past Carmody's classroom what had become of the bold persecutor of communists. Matt was still examining the book, an ancient, illustrated copy of *Hamlet*, when Carmody appeared.

'What did he want?' he asked, his face protruding, eyes agog, making his head appear like a comic effigy of itself. There was, however, a deference in the way he spoke, something Matt had observed over the previous few days, leading him to think Carmody had somehow or other got wind of the encounter with Costigan and Dixie and was treading carefully.

'He came about the auditions he's having on Monday.' Matt held up the book. Carmody moved closer to examine it.

'An odd fish.' He hesitated, looked quizzically at Matt for a moment. 'Mind you, in all fairness he hasn't caused any trouble, not like the man he's replacing, here every other friggen day, flinging catechism questions around like, like I don't know what.' He unclenched his closed fist as if to release something into the air.

'How long will he be gone for? I mean why is he gone?'

Carmody scrutinized Matt as if to imply he knew the answer, then tensing to the sound of a shrill screech from his own classroom, charged back up the hall.

'*Hamlet*,' Matt whispered, hoping that too few would turn up to stage a production, but instantly abandoning that hope when it struck him that Madelene could get a part, that he could accompany her home after practices, a thought which shot across the horizon like a sizzling fuse wire illuminating the entire winter.

.*

On Saturday morning, when Matt, on his way to Colls' to collect Madelene, opened the front door, a sack of anthracite fell in with a thud. It had been left there sometime during the night by Con O' Leary, a publican who sidelined in black market goods. He had undertaken to supply Mrs Sheridan with four hundredweight bags of this very scarce Aga fuel and had, as part of the arrangement, been paid in advance. In the event he could only supply one hundredweight. Keen to get going, but prevented from closing the door by the sprawling bag, Matt considered manoeuvring it out onto the doorstep with his foot. That would mean leaving the job for Mrs Sheridan. So there was, in effect, little choice but to cart the bag through the house to the shed at the end of the garden. Alerted by the kafuffle, Mrs Sheridan rushed out of the kitchen, saw him staggering towards her with the bag held at arm's length, grabbed a bundle of old newspapers from under the stairs and began to spread them on the floor in front of him.

'It's a question of integrity, really,' she pronounced testily. 'Leaving it just like that at the hall door. And at night. As though I wouldn't see the dishonesty of it. I can assure you it wouldn't have happened if Benny was alive.' Words

Matt angrily dismissed when he saw that the black, liquidy slack had leaked down the front of his trousers. He left the bag down to examine the damage.

'Oh goodness. They'll have to be steeped straight away.' Mrs Sheridan raised her hands as though under arrest.

'May as well get this done first.' He hoisted the bag up and, holding it as far out as possible, staggered down the overgrown garden path, kicked the rickety shed door open and dumped it in the nearest space available. Once back inside, he charged up to his room, changed, charged down again, his trousers rolled into a bundle, ready to be immersed in the basin Mrs Sheridan was filling at the sink.

'So slow, this tap.'

'I have to go. I'll leave these here.' He scrambled out the door to where he'd left Evelyn Sheridan's bicycle which he'd arranged with Mrs Sheridan to borrow.

When he arrived at Colls breathless after ten minutes of furious pedalling, Madelene was already at the top of the lane, waiting. The instant she saw him she cycled off in the direction of the Abbey, her back arched over the frame of her bike, head down, her weight shifting effortlessly from one hip to the other.

'Come on, hurry,' words that trailed behind her like a kite tail as she pressed forward. Soon Matt was gathering speed, intent on passing her, which he didn't manage to do until they were freewheeling down Baily's Hill, going faster and faster, her hair rising and falling behind her as though she was swimming underwater.

Once ahead he slowed down, then eased to a limby dawdle, anticipating that she would draw up beside him, exhausted. He felt triumphant waiting there, so when she just shot past, head still down, he immediately leapt up on his bike and brought every ounce of his weight to bear on the highest of the pedals, determined to overtake and leave her so far behind that she'd abandon all hope of outpacing him. The solid clank, which sounded just as he pressed the pedal down, was unmistakable. 'Fuck,' he muttered. Not only had the chain come off but it had got tightly furled and was jammed solidly between the axle and the metal guard. It didn't unlock with a back pedal, neither did it move when, down on his knees he tried to release it. The tool kit purse, hooked to the back of the saddle, was empty except for some sweet papers. He looked about for a stick. The seconds were ticking by and with them the possibility of catching up with her. Maybe she'll realize something has happened and turn back, a hope that kept him glancing up from the slow, filthy job of releasing and refitting the chain. She didn't. Then, just when he'd put the last link in place and was gearing up to cycle like the clappers, he heard the creak and squeal of a bike approaching from behind; two bikes as it turned out.

Madelene's aunts ground to an unsteady halt a few yards away, their goggley concern radiating towards Matt in oppressive waves. He considered just belting off, a plan that wavered for a moment before it withered to a wish.

'Chain came off, Madelene doesn't know, have to catch up with her.' He leapt onto the bike. But his explanation was too hurried, or so they gave him to believe, because they began to repeat it to each other, laboriously filling in the gaps.

'The chain came off Mr Duggan's bicycle. Madelene was cycling ahead and didn't realize what had happened,' Statia explained to Rose, her words charged with wonder and pronounced as though they were being read to a child from a story book.

'But it's back on now. He's put the chain back on. Look.' They both smiled at him, creating a gap into which several thoughts rushed headlong, among them the notion that

Madelene had not been racing him. She was fleeing from them, which is why she dashed away the second he arrived.

Rose and Statia had positioned their bicycles in such a way as to fence him in. There was nothing for it except to edge forward until they moved out of the way.

'Meet you there,' Statia said as he slid out through the narrow gap he'd forced them to create. 'Meet you there,' Rose echoed.

A few moments on Matt looked back, finding them, as he supposed he would, following behind. Their get-ups, however peculiar when they were off their bikes, looked altogether bizarre as they cycled along, each of them sitting up straight and holding the handlebars as they might a wheel barrow. They must, he thought, have a dressing-up box. He imagined a large chest into which they delved like children, unearthing outfits. What stood out most, as the distance between him and them grew, was the beekeeper's hat, complete with insect-proof netting, that Statia had on. When he'd first seen it, a few minutes earlier, he thought it might be to protect against midges, which later in the day would shoal the air in their millions. But when he'd looked down and seen her tasselled, hand-knitted Aran socks, the notion that she had been guided by some practical consideration just went by the board. Rose, less flamboyant, was wearing a tweed russet-coloured man's jacket, with a chunky Tara brooch replica pinned to the collar.

The closer he got to the Abbey the more irked he became by them. It galled him to think that they would be there trooping behind himself and Madelene all morning, stalking about like ostriches, watching everything they did. Bad enough going to an abbey in the first place, he thought, but going with two harum-scarum chaperones was the bitter end. It cast such a dark cloud over the day that he began to project forward to the next time he would meet Madelene. And beyond that, to the train out of Rathisland, building up speed in his mind, soon to arrive in Kingsbridge, gateway to the crowded, anonymous streets of Dublin.

He wheeled his bike across the field separating the Abbey from the road, all the while looking this way and that, sure Madelene was going to emerge any minute. The buildings, a small, roofless chapel, a tall round tower, and in between, a partly enclosed courtyard with the remains of a cloister running down one side, were a lot more derelict than Matt had anticipated.

'Madelene,' he called out, then again, much louder.

'Here, down here.' Her voice came from the graveyard beside the Abbey.

He slipped through the metal turnstile and raced down the overgrown path. Suddenly, her hand shot out from behind a large, upright headstone, where she was crouched. She grasped his arm and began to shake it, demanding to know where he'd left his bike.

'Just up there.' he pointed in the direction of the turnstile.

'Quick. Go back and hide it.' She let go his arm.

'Quick, before they come.' Her head shook as she spoke.

When he returned, she pointed to the space beside her, moving over a fraction. He crouched down, manoeuvred himself in. Her head was pressed against the gravestone, her eyes lightly closed. Her expression could, he thought, be one of annoyance, exasperation with her aunts. But the angle at which her head was tilted, the few stray strands of hair on her forehead, her skin, her breathing, had a kind of magnetism, that independently, or almost independently, drew his hand towards her cheek, so entranced now, that the distant voices scratching at the periphery of the moment, seemed unreal at first.

'You go. Tell them you haven't found me yet.' Madelene sprung forward as though waking from a disturbing dream.

Matt's outstretched hand fell limply by his side.

He leapt up, rushed to the entrance to the graveyard where Rose and Statia were making their way through the turnstile together. By the time he reached them they had managed to get stuck, so his plan to direct them back up to the Abbey to search for Madelene had to be postponed until he freed them. They followed his instructions with a mixture of alarm and incredulity, their puzzled expressions turning first to relief, then to triumph when, with their hands raised above their heads, they eventually made it into the graveyard.

'Have you seen Madelene?' Matt rushed the question at them.

They looked at each other.

'We thought …'

'I'm sure she's here, somewhere,' Matt interrupted, attempting, while he spoke, to usher them back through the turnstile and up to the Abbey.

'No, no.' Rose covered her lips with her loosely spread fingers. 'It's too dangerous going back through that.'

'Yes, too dangerous.' Statia echoed, pointing at the gate at the other end of the cemetery, indicating they should leave that way.

'Looks a bit soggy around the gate,' Matt warned in a loud, theatrical voice, expecting to see Madelene emerge from behind the headstone any second. Down they trundled, periodically gripping each other's forearms as though on ice, so intent on making it appear like a dangerous expedition that they walked right past the headstone. Matt, following behind, slowed down as he approached it, preparing to tell Madelene he'd meet her inside the Abbey, but she was no longer there.

'Here, Matt, up here.'

He turned, scanned the enclosure, his attention rapidly travelling to the top of the tower. In a matter of minutes he was scrambling up the tower steps, soon to arrive at the top.

'I knew it. I knew it would be like this.' In a bid to impress on him how vigilant Rose and Statia were, Madelene looked anxiously over Matt's shoulder. He moved forward, drew her hands together and enfolded them in his.

'If you close your eyes, they'll go away.'

Madeline smiled a little as she closed her eyes. Matt raised his hands and cupped her cheeks, then moved slowly towards her, feeling her move a little towards him. He allowed his hands to slip around until they cradled her head. He could feel her breath on his lips, a sensation that prompted him to dawdle at the precipice of a kiss, brushing his lips against hers, continuing until every fibre yearned for that kiss. Everything gave way to the heady, flash lightning sensations that generated. Even Rose and Statia's voices, all the while getting closer, had a reverie-like quality, remaining aimless and lost at the edge of the all encompassing world in which Matt and Madelene found themselves. And there they remained long after both opened their eyes to see if what had happened, what was happening, was as affecting, as profoundly affecting, as both felt it was.

When Matt eventually spoke, his voice sounded a little hoarse.

'Father Finn is doing a play.' He cleared his throat.

'U-hoo, up there.'

'Father Finn is putting on a play. *Hamlet.* Practices are on Mondays in the parochial house. You'll come, won't you?' Matt asked, his hands now enveloping hers again.

'Yes, but don't collect me. I'll get there by myself.'

'Here you are.' Rose, pushing her way into the already

crowded space, forced Matt down onto the last step.

'My goodness. What a climb. Oh, but look. Look at the view. Statia, Look here. Look.'

Statia gazed across the rolling landscape, then pointed towards a distant farm house.

'Is that Thompsons of Ardfinnan?' She turned to Madelene, 'We used to go to such lovely parties there when we were young. Such lovely parties.'

For the remainder of the time they spent at the Abbey, Madelene, followed closely by Matt, climbed over walls, picked her way across narrow ledges, ducked in and out of the cloister doorways, every so often calling to her aunts to follow. And they did, but at a much slower pace, stumbling over dislodged stones, stopping here and there to regain their composure, steering each other up and down steps, all the while driven on by images of Mary Teehan, certain as they called out after Madelene, that history was repeating itself under their very noses.

'I've never been in a play,' Madelene said as she and Matt freewheeled down the road leading away from the Abbey.

'You don't have to be in it if you don't want. There's lots to putting on a play besides being in it.'

'Oh I don't mind being in it. I'd quite like it really.' Madelene looked back at her aunts who, leaning forward over their bicycles, were visibly straining to keep pace. She began to slow down, waiting for them to catch up. Before long all four were cycling at a slow, even pace, a foursome that remained together until they reached the top of Colls' lane.

Chapter 10

On the evening of the first play practice Matt found himself sitting beside Mrs Sheridan on one of the dozen or so spoon-backed chairs loosely arranged in a circle in the parochial house drawing-room. To his right, all spruced up and barely recognisable without his shop coat, was Tony Lehane, the draper who every morning hooked frocks and coats to the outside bar of his shop awning as Matt passed on his way to school.

'I can't see us doing that.' He pointed to Mrs Sheridan's copy of *Hamlet*.

'I think he's his mind made up.' Matt nodded in Father Finn's direction, then leaned back as Mrs Sheridan stretched across to say something, confidentially it appeared, to Tony Lehane. 'It's a wonderful play, but not for such a mixed group. I mean, so many different tastes.' She looked around the room, allowing the sweep of her gaze to slow down as she reached the two ruddy-faced women chatting opposite them.

'From what I know everyone dies at the end. Hardly what you'd call Christmas entertainment?' He turned to

Matt for confirmation. But Matt, on high alert waiting for Madelene to arrive, was only partly paying attention. 'Think so,' he said, his sights remaining fixed on the door as he spoke. She probably waited until the last minute to tell her aunts she was coming, he figured, then just dashed out the door, making sure they didn't come along.

'They all die in the end. Don't they?' Tony Lehane said to Mrs Sheridan, his round, glossy face eager, expectant. She looked at him blankly, repositioned herself on her chair, now conspicuously anxious to pay attention to Father Finn who'd just clapped his hands in a bid for quiet. Smiling broadly, he assured everyone that the parts he was about to allocate were temporary, 'Just to get things started.' Miss Dunne, his housekeeper, decked out in a royal-blue pleated party frock, began nodding as soon as he spoke and didn't stop until he'd finished. She turned to her brother John Bosco and in a hissy gush of excitement started to explain what had been said. Just then, the doorknocker sounded. She sprung up like a jack-in-the-box, but didn't go to answer it, impressing on everyone that there was a definite protocol to be followed. The knocker sounded again, thunderingly loud this time. Eventually, she minced her way across the room, her expression growing more severe as she went.

The instant Matt heard Madelene's voice his whole face tingled with a burning sensation

'Ah, the fair Ophelia,' Father Finn announced as soon as she appeared in the doorway. He gripped the waistband of his short-sleeved, blackberry-stitch pullover, tugging it down several times to extend it further than it could go. One of his cufflinks caught the light, creating a cipher of rapidly moving glints on the wall and the ceiling. Madelene pirouetted around as she took off her coat, then stood holding it, sort of hugging it, as she looked about for somewhere to put it. She twirled again, holding it even closer, the whole scene moving like a merry-go-round, coming to a standstill when Miss Dunne stepped forward and took the coat from her. 'Thanks,' Madelene said, smiling as she surveyed the group. Matt thought she was about to speak, maybe apologize for the disruption her late arrival was causing. Instead, she made her way over to where he was sitting, lifting her hair from her collar before she flicked it back. He lowered his head, embarrassed at being singled out by her in this public way, steeling himself to tell her it wasn't funny as soon as she came close enough.

'Madelene, Madelene Coll,' he heard her say confidently to Mrs Sheridan, 'we've not met but Matt's told me all about you.'

When eventually he chanced to look up she was beaming in his direction, a sassiness to her smile, making it clear she was well aware of the waves she was creating. He lowered his head again, hoping she would see how uncomfortable he was.

'Can I call you Hilda?' She said with such feigned naïveté that Mrs Sheridan, whose Christian name Matt had never heard spoken, simply said, 'Please.' Madelene smiled at everyone in the room and returned to her chair.

Though discomfited by her carry-on, there was a sense in which Matt enjoyed it. Whenever, in the days that followed, he drifted into thinking about her, he would smile at the cool-headed entrance she'd made, at the way she swung into the room, everything about her, how she held her coat, how she stood in the middle of the room, twirling, and the way she could debunk things while appearing to do the opposite.

Meanwhile, Mrs Sheridan, who was, *sotto voce*, rehearsing Gertrude, Hamlet's mother's lines, in preparation for the moment when she would have to say them aloud, glowered at Father Finn, straining to conceal her annoyance when, without as much as a single glance at the text, he delivered them all. And that's how it continued, with little or no opening given to anyone to read the parts he'd allocated to them. It was, in effect, a one-man show, passionate, flamboyant, intense and ultimately exhausting.

'Well, there you have it, the main part, Ophelia,' Matt said, when at the end of the evening, in a bid to avoid leaving with the others, they'd offered to help Miss Dunne to replace the chairs.

'It's a gorgeous name, Ophelia. But I didn't twig what she's like?' Madelene crinkled her nose. 'Even who she is, to be honest.'

'She's Hamlet's … well, hard to say really. The impression at the beginning is that he's mad about her. Or was, at any rate.'

'You mean, he … they're sweethearts?'

'Yes. And, no.'

'Mmm … I see.' Madelene darted a covert glance in Miss Dunne's direction.

'I couldn't play a part that has anything like that going on with him,' she blurted as soon as they were outside. 'He gives me the creeps, all those faces he keeps pulling.'

'Father Finn?' Matt laughed.

'Oh God.' Her arm shot out like a level crossing barrier, bringing Matt to a complete standstill.

Directly opposite the gates, Statia and Rose, their bicycles resting against a lamppost, were waving frantically, hopping up and down as though they'd been shipwrecked and had just spotted a rescue vessel.

Without saying a word to each other, Madelene and Matt ducked in behind the great cedar to their right. But too flustered to take advantage of being alone and out of sight, they just stood there awkwardly, waiting to be discovered.

'U-hoo. U-hoo.' Rose and Statia's voices grew nearer and nearer.

'Tomorrow evening after tea. Top of the lane,' Matt whispered as they stepped forward to join her aunts, hardly pausing before he wished them a firm 'Good evening'.

'So dark,' Statia said, infusing the words with mystery.

'Exceptionally so,' Rose replied, striking an opposite note, 'we couldn't tell if you saw us or not.'

'Yes. We couldn't tell if you saw us or not,' Statia chimed in.

'Very dark, alright.' Matt agreed, wondering if they could go on talking about the darkness indefinitely.

*

A few days later, at the top of the lane, where they had arranged to meet unknown to her aunts, Madelene, who'd been piecing the plot of the play together in a comical sort of way, brought up the question of Ophelia again.

'Was she beautiful?' she asked.

'You mean, is she meant to be beautiful?'

'Yes, was she beautiful?'

'Definitely. That's why you got the part.' Matt smiled, swung her around, drew her towards him. 'Oh, no,' he said, looking over her shoulder and down the lane. 'It's them.' Madelene froze.

'Why don't we just stay like this? See what they say?' He drew her closer, so close that she began to suspect he might be joking.

'If you're …'

He burst out laughing, allowed himself to be pushed away, laughing so much that he began to fall about, prompting Madelene to point at him, laughing herself, both heading for each other in clownish, stumbling movements. Matt, still laughing, put his arms around her. She drew back; 'Shush,' she whispered, 'or they really will come.' She took his arms and placed them firmly by his side.

'Why do they follow you everywhere?'

'I'm beginning to think it's funny, really.' Madelene smiled indulgently.

'I suppose it is, in a way.'

'I've told them they needn't worry, that I'm able to look after myself.'

'And what did they say to that?'

'Nothing, that's the point. They don't say anything. They just look worried.' She laughed nervously, 'Dad said not to let me out of their sight and they are taking him at his word. I don't want to say it to him, not in a letter anyway, and it looks now as if I won't be seeing him until December, when he gets leave.'

'And your mother, will she be home then as well?'

'It's hard to know with Mum,' and in the same breath, 'I have to go.'

'Wait, wait a minute …' Matt called out, but she was already well on her way, gathering pace as she went. He was bewildered by the suddenness of her departure. He tried to make sense of it, focusing on what he thought was a slight tremor in her voice when she said she had to go. But there was no understanding it. He resolved to ask her about it after the practice on Monday, ask her if something he'd said had upset her. But when the time came he didn't mention it, partly because there was no sign of anything being amiss, but mainly because he'd come to believe that she'd just panicked at the thought of her aunts showing up.

As the practices progressed, Statia and Rose came to accept that it was not possible to supervise Madelene's every move. Determining when the practices ended, so as to be there when she emerged, was one of the difficulties. The worsening weather was another. So too was Madelene's own dissatisfaction, frequently conveyed in the form of assurances about her safety. The upshot was more, a good deal more, unsupervised time.

*

As the weeks went by the cast became increasingly disgruntled with the way the play was going. It wasn't very obvious at the outset, just an occasional loud sigh and a little shifting about on the creaky chairs. In this mute, awkward way the cast gradually managed to express their frustration with Father Finn's one-man show. Mrs Sheridan confided to Matt that she wasn't sure if his reading all the parts himself was the correct approach, but added, that it was 'probably necessary'. She didn't say 'probably necessary because of literacy levels'. But she may as well have, because by that stage Matt was almost as well attuned to what she didn't say as to what she did. This was particularly so when it came to Madelene. Despite the many opportunities he gave her to say something complimentary, she never did.

She continued, though more tacitly, to voice her support for Father Finn's approach to the play, so it came as a surprise to Matt and to Madelene too, when about halfway through the fifth rehearsal, her voice was first to sound in what turned out to be a full-scale coup.

'I mean for goodness' sake, what age is he?' She spoke indignantly, cutting across Father Finn who, without reference to the text, was acting out an exchange between Hamlet and his mother. Initially, he took the interruption as a compliment, regarding it as a measure of how gripped Mrs Sheridan was by his performance. He smiled.

'Hamlet's behaviour is ridiculous.' She moved to the edge of her chair, creating a wave of righteousness that acted as a call to arms. At least that's how it appeared because everyone else, except Miss Dunne and John Bosco, moved to the edge of their chairs too.

'His age? Hamlet's age?' Father Finn looked around the room, puzzled as to why everyone appeared as eager for the answer as Mrs Sheridan.

'Well thirty, or so.'

'Worse than I thought.' Mrs Sheridan looked to the rest of the group. 'I don't know how anyone else feels about this, but I think it's ridiculous. He's a grown man and he's behaving like a seven-year-old. When Benny died, my daughter Evelyn wasn't even able to get home …' She drew breath fiercely. '… I mean there's a war. It's ludicrous. I …' She stopped suddenly as though frightened by the course her challenge was taking. She raised her chin, angled her head abruptly to one side in a bid for composure. Almost everyone in the room was offering agreement in one form or another, nodding, mumbling, smiling sympathetically at her, a wave of support that prompted Tony Lehane to speak out, 'She's right, Father. What with the way things are we'd be better off doing a variety show. Something to get a bit of a laugh.'

What did he mean? Matt wondered. Was he referring to the Emergency? To the way Father Finn was conducting the practices? To the difficulties people were having following *Hamlet*?

Either way, it mattered little, because he was addressing a group who, in the course of five meetings had sat through two and a half readings of *Hamlet* and were now at breaking point. 'Yes,' a half-dozen voices sounded before he'd even finished speaking, some following through with, 'He's right', many of them saying 'yes' again, louder, to keep the momentum going. Father Finn placed his thumb and index finger forcibly on his forehead, just as he did when he recited the soliloquies, then swung around to face Madelene.

'A variety show?' His jaw slackened.

'I don't know, really.' She looked to Matt.

The possibility that Father Finn could, at any moment, burst into tears crossed Matt's mind but only briefly, because all at once his face hardened. He turned to the group, a petulance about him now that made his overly good manners seem contrived, a way of imposing his will. Thoughts that scattered the instant Matt heard him say, 'Mr Duggan?'

Matt tried to create the impression he didn't know what he was being asked to consider.

'It is, as I'm sure Mr Duggan will agree … ' He gestured extravagantly to Matt, '… the greatest play ever written?' Matt inhaled deeply. A smell of cooking suet, faintly discernable in the room earlier, had grown stronger, throwing all the other odours into sharp relief; Mrs Sheridan's face powder, Tony Lehane's hair oil, turf smoke and the colourless anonymity of the room which, by association, evoked that vaguely surgical smell found in doctors' and dentists' waiting rooms.

'It wouldn't mean the end of *Hamlet* altogether,' Matt heard Tony Lehane say from what sounded like a long distance away. 'It could be built into a variety show. A few excerpts that you'd recite.' Tony leaned out from his chair, one arm extended in Father Finn's direction, a plea to have his suggestion considered. As before, everyone made some sort of an agreement sound, not least Mrs Sheridan, who, when the surge of accord died down, assured Father Finn he'd 'steal the show' with his performance of the soliloquies. Then, more or less in the same breath, asked how many there were in the play.

'Five,' he said, exhaling loudly before slouching back on his chair. Instantly, she and Tony Lehane decided that all five soliloquies could be delivered at separate points in the show. 'A main act split into five,' as Tony Lehane put it. Mrs Sheridan, now smiling with a kind of strained delicacy, asked Father Finn how long they would take to perform, quickly following through with the suggestion that he might time himself reading them.

It never occurred to Matt to question her sudden abandonment of *Hamlet*, or indeed her equally sudden enthusiasm for a variety show. At least not until afterwards when walking Madelene home, she pointed out that Mrs Sheridan had included five piano pieces, one after each soliloquy, to be performed by her daughter Evelyn, expected home from the Basel Conservatoire for Christmas.

'Can you see it?' Madelene said springing out of the crook of his arm, then turning around and walking backwards as she ran her fingers up and down imaginary piano keys, her eyes tightly shut, her head swinging abruptly from side to side. Matt tiptoed past her undetected, clasped her waist from behind, causing her to shriek loudly. The breathless laughter that followed had a shuddery edge, a sensation to which they abandoned themselves in the way children telling ghost stories might abandon themselves to fear.

Afterwards, long afterwards, whenever Matt tried to recall when he first told Madelene he loved her, that evening came to mind. But he could never be fully sure, because as soon as it did, the many other evenings on the Castle Wall Road would flood in, all merging until there was only one evening, Madelene and himself sailing along, accountable to each other only, sole occupants of a world that held nothing but happiness.

*

The moment it became clear that *Hamlet* had been successfully supplanted, Tony Lehane whipped out the hand-written sketch from the inside pocket of his jacket for what, all along, he'd been hoping would be the mainstay of the 1942 Rathisland Variety Show. He had been kingpin of Rathisland Christmas variety shows for many years, so his restoration was widely welcomed. He began to outline the sketch; the main character, Windy, was, he explained, so named 'on account of his stomach'. The laughter, tittery, intermittent and high-pitched at first, developed like a choral work in which a soprano takes an initial lead and is gradually joined by a range of other voices. Soon the reading was drowned out by laughter, loud, loose laughter creating its own unstoppable momentum. Every time he tried to continue, a new wave of laughter just cascaded forward and swept his words away.

The show began to take shape rapidly, soon on course for its three-day-run in mid December. The only difficulty remaining was the length. It was, when all the individual party pieces were included, over three hours long; it had to be cut back. Tony Lehane suggested that Father Finn's recital of the soliloquies and the piano pieces could be staged together, conjuring up an image of piano music wafting across the stage while Father Finn delivered his lines. No one responded, creating an atmosphere in which Mrs Sheridan could, after a moment or two, say, 'I think not,' without having to take it any further. In the end a number of other individual performances were merged together, resulting in a dozen or so performers, some reluctantly, others enthusiastically, singing along, meandering medley of their party pieces, including, 'Daisy, Daisy', 'Báidín Fheidhlimid', 'A Long Way to Tipperary', 'Three Little Maids', 'Eibhlín a Rún', all accompanied by blind Billy Foyle on the spoons, and arranged to encourage the audience to sing along.

Matt's classes were to lead into the national anthem at the end, which left him with little to do during the practices themselves. And Madelene, in charge of make-up and costumes, was equally at a loose end. They continued to turn up, but left earlier and earlier, taking the Rectory Road, the long way back to Colls: long, long evenings, always star-spangled, a permanent backdrop to the world they had created.

*

Out of the blue, less than a week before the opening night, Mrs Sheridan announced that if the show went ahead as planned it would be a shambles. She insisted that a lot more work was necessary, that the sketches lacked finesse, that the sing-along medley was rough at the edges, that the lighting for the soliloquies was all wrong, in short, coming up with so many criticisms that when she suggested it shouldn't open until a week later than scheduled, the cast, though not particularly enthusiastic about the change, went along with it.

But Madelene, who'd already had plans in place to travel back to London would, if the change was put in place, now miss the show.

'I can't. I'm going …' she began, instantly cut short by Mrs Sheridan, who, smiling statically, told her not to worry, adding that a replacement to do the make-up and costumes could easily be found.

'That woman gives me the pip. I don't know how you can live under the same roof as her,' Madelene said as soon as they left.

'In fairness, there was a good bit of truth in what she said.' Matt hoped it would end at that.

'I'm glad I won't be there. It's bad enough watching her bossing everyone now, but she's going to be much worse at the real thing.'

'You're probably right,' Matt said as disinterestedly as he could, relieved that the moment seemed to be passing. He didn't want to add fuel to Madelene's dislike of Mrs Sheridan, which is what would have happened had he told her he suspected Mrs Sheridan had changed the opening date because of the difficulty Evelyn was having in getting home. The boat she was scheduled to take from Bordeaux to Cobh, organized months beforehand, was cancelled due to the increasing risk to commercial and passenger shipping in the Atlantic. Finding an alternative had turned out to be exceptionally difficult. In the end, Mrs Sheridan had to go to Dublin to make what, by any reckoning, turned out to be very piecemeal arrangements. The journey involved going to Lisbon, then overland to Le Havre and from there to Cobh on a Spanish cargo vessel. And it was going to take the best part of a week, which meant that she would not be back in time to perform if the show opened as originally planned.

*

On the afternoon Madelene was due to catch the boat train, the first stage of her journey home, Matt set both his classes work to do, then went to the middle window to watch out for her. Travelling to the station with Dixie and her aunts, he calculated she would pass by the school somewhere between quarter and half past two. He opened the window and stood with his back to the class waiting. Behind him, the pupils made shivery noises, some of them drawing breath sharply as though battling with icy winds.

Just after two thirty, still looking out the window, he heard, though he was not sure at first, the clippidy-clop approach of a pony and trap. He swung around to face the class.

'If I hear as much as one more sound from anyone, everyone will stay in for an extra half-hour.' He swung back, his interest in what was going on outside now the intense focus of all the pupils. One, two, then a few more, chanced standing up to investigate. Just at that point, Madelene, all wrapped up in what Matt supposed were Statia and Rose's furs, and travelling at a pace through the thinning fog, blew a kiss in his direction. A loud kissing noise sounded behind him, then the whole room filled with kissing noises, soon interspersed with sucking, slurpy moans and sighs. Matt's cheeks began to burn. He wanted desperately to turn around, but knew his deep, scarlet colour would only make things worse. He waited, hoping that the cold December air would cool his face enough to confront the class and demand silence. Before he'd managed to make a move, however, that silence had descended, sharp and fast as a guillotine. He swung around, looked at the motionless pupils, then at the door where Carmody was standing.

'*Cheapas nach raibh éinne anseo,*' 'I thought there was no one here,' words that shot across the room, pinning Matt to the spot, no explanation to offer. Carmody glared at the pupils, then left. Matt closed the window.

*

From the moment the curtain went up on the opening night of the show Matt found himself revising his expectations of how it would go. It wasn't just the continuous, often ribald exchanges between the audience and the performers that forced that revision, but the many impromptu sideshows that sprung up in the aisles. These brief re-enactments of the action on stage, performed mainly by children, involved mimicking a scene, or a few lines, or sometimes just a series of gestures. In general, little or no distinction was drawn between performers and audience. Everybody was there to enjoy themselves regardless of what happened on stage or in the auditorium. It didn't particularly matter that Evelyn was too exhausted after her journey to play on that first night, or that when, on the following night, she did play, she had to use the ancient piano because the baby grand, which had taken Matt and four others half the day to move from Mrs Sheridan's drawing-room to the parochial hall, didn't fit down the narrow passage leading into the auditorium.

The one part of the show that did command partial silence was Father Finn's delivery of the soliloquies. His entrance on stage in a black leotard, complete with a large silver medallion was greeted with a cacophony of yelps, whoops, yaps, catcalls and piercing whistles. He walked to the front of the stage, folded his arms and with a deeply dejected look about him, waited until there was silence. Then, all at once, he dug his index finger and his thumb into his forehead and inhaled loudly. An excruciatingly long pause followed before he released, 'To be or not to be.' Matt couldn't decide if the audience was dumbfounded or embarrassed, a mix of both he figured, which intensified when Father Finn flung Hamlet's dilemma at them with both hands, went down on bended knee to plead with fate, darted to the back of the stage to brood in the half-light, then leapt forward to exclaim, 'Ay, there's the rub.' In the end he collapsed centre stage like a deflating mannequin. Well over a minute passed before the audience realized the recital had ended. When they did, they clapped wildly, an expression of relief for the most part, which little by little took on a sing-song rhythm, soon to become a rowdy parody of an enthusiastic response. Father Finn, however, took it to be the real thing and bowed dozens of times before finally backing off the stage.

'It all worked out well. I mean everyone enjoyed it,' Matt said to Evelyn, when after the final performance he'd remained behind to help Mrs Sheridan bring a variety of props back to the house.

'Yes. Looked like that, though I can't say it's my sort of thing.'

'The piano is a bit on the shaky side.'

'It was perfect. Perfect. Out of tune. Missing notes.' She laughed. 'Mummy wanted to have it tuned when our own piano didn't fit, but that would have made it worse.' She laughed again.

Condescending, Matt thought, but laughed all the same, trying, as he'd done from the start, to be as friendly as possible. She was every bit as good-looking as she appeared in the photograph on the mantelpiece. Her movements, like those of a ballet dancer, were neat and highly co-ordinated. And she had a great range of facial expressions, most of which came into play, even in the shortest of encounters. But she was, Matt felt, something of a poser, always trying to appear older than her age; twenty, soon to be twenty-one. He was none-theless intrigued and inclined, sometimes, to stare at her; her black couture costume with its sleek sealskin collar, her magazine figure and her foreign antics; kissing her mother on both cheeks almost every time they met, pursing her scarlet lips for no apparent reason, holding her teacup between the extreme edge of her thumb and her forefinger. Very affected, he thought, but it also occurred to him, more than once, that she might not be as self-assured as she seemed.

On her first afternoon home, she'd appeared in the doorway of the bedroom she shared with her mother and, pressing the palm of her hand against her forehead, said to Matt; 'If you don't mind, I must ask you to make less noise going up and down the stairs.'

'I don't mind at all,' he said, adding that he was 'very sorry'. Neither did he mind the way she stopped, often abruptly, whatever conversation she was having with her mother as soon as he appeared. Even the sharpness with which she'd told him to be careful when he was manoeuvring the piano out the front door hadn't particularly bothered him. These would-be slights, however, all came bounding back when, the evening after the final performance, Mrs Sheridan, on her way out to a meeting, asked Evelyn if she'd mind serving Matt his supper.

She stared crossly at her mother.

'It's in the lower oven, fully prepared.'

Evelyn's stare intensified.

'I can get it myself,' Matt smiled, but Evelyn and Mrs Sheridan remained at daggers drawn.

'I'm sure Evelyn ...'

'I don't see why we have to have a bloody lodger,' Evelyn shot an accusing look at Mrs Sheridan, then stormed out of the room.

'I blame myself really,' Mrs Sheridan said quietly to Matt a moment or two after the bedroom door slammed overhead. 'I ought to have told her about you before she arrived home. This is completely out of character, you know. She's such a sweet, good girl normally.'

'I'm sure,' Matt said, confounding Mrs Sheridan, who'd not heard him speak ironically before.

Chapter 11

Walking slowly through Balbriggan, his Gladstone swinging by his side, Matt took in everything in the same dawdling way he used to do on his way home from school; the long row of hanging hams in Colliers, the smell of saltpetre, the damped sawdust around the door, Mr Collier's Santa Claus cheeks, his shop coat sleeves extending halfway up his stocky arms as he spread a large sheet of brown paper on the counter. And Dollards, the hardware store, its door slightly ajar, a mix of paraffin and creosote drifting out into the cold afternoon air, Mr Dollard's long pale face, even longer and paler than he recalled.

'The prodigal returns!' Hugh shouted from upstairs, pounding his way down, angling his shoulder to jostle Matt, giving him a moment to step to the side, laughing before he began to mimic their aunt Agnes; 'Well, honest to God, you're getting as big as a house.'

Matt was so pleased to be home that he couldn't bring himself to say anything. He fixed on the ancient orange star hooked around the hall light, conduit to a great swell of childhood Christmases.

'How are you anyway?' Hugh brought his fist to bear in slow motion on Matt's shoulder.

'I'm fine. Couldn't be better.'

'I hope you're hungry, 'cos the fatted calf has been prepared in your honour.'

Hugh led the way into the kitchen where their mother, midway between the cooker and the sink carrying a large, steaming saucepan, stopped in her tracks.

'I didn't hear you coming. You're early.'

'The train wasn't as late as I thought it was going to be.' Matt left down his bag.

'Take that upstairs,' she said to Hugh, nodding at the Gladstone through the billowing steam.

'No,' Matt cut in. 'No, I'll bring it up myself.'

'Take it up for him. Go on.'

'Here. Give it to me.' Hugh went to take the bag.

'I'm well able to bring it up by myself.'

'It's an order from on high.' Hugh bowed from the waist down in the direction of their mother.

'Where's Will?'

'He's staying behind.' His mother's voice strained as she leaned over the sink to drain the saucepan of potatoes. 'Brother Doyle offered to take a few of them, the good ones, for extra classes.' She straightened up. 'He'll be here in a few minutes.'

'The joys of Euclid,' Hugh sighed.

Before long Matt was sitting in his usual place while his mother hovered in the background, quietly pleased at the gusto with which they were all tucking into their food. And, biding her time until she could top up their diminishing pyramids of mashed potatoes, she plied Matt with question about his routine. How long does it take to walk to the school? What kind of suppers does he get? Where was the other teacher, Mr Canning, from?

'It's a pain not having the BBC,' Matt said, interrupting Hugh and Will who had begun to discuss the war.

'Can you never get it?' Will asked.

'Well sometimes, but so crackly that you wouldn't be bothered listening in. Hard to understand when you think that programmes can be got from Berlin. And Irish language ones at that.'

'You're joking?'

'No. I heard it. Loud and clear. Much clearer than the BBC.'

'Jesus,' Hugh exclaimed, 'the Germans deserve to win the war.'

'I'll not have the Holy Name used in vain in this house,' their mother's voice from over beside the sink.

'Sorry, Mam,' Hugh quipped sardonically.

'It's not me you have to say sorry to. It's the Lord.'

'Sorry, Lord.' Hugh raised his eyes. 'Go on. Say what you were saying about the Irish broadcasts.

'Yeah. There's this fellow that has a short wave. Battery run, because he's out the country. But there's a roof aerial, the lot. It's all propaganda that's being put out. Anti-British stuff. Saying the things they did here in the past, trying to make sure we don't side with his Majesty. Balbriggan was mentioned.'

'You're joking.'

'Yeah. It said that English military cadets, with the police from the town and the Black and Tans, broke into some-one's shop here and beat him to death. That they dragged him to the barracks and that two others had been killed as well, bayoneted to death and left in the gutter. Twenty-five houses in the town were supposed to have been set on fire. It said everyone left and hid in ditches and drains outside the town until the Black and Tans and the cadets left. They made it sound like it really happened. 'Course I was able to tell them it didn't.'

'It did,' their mother said emphatically.

'It didn't?' Words Matt inflected to sound like a question.

'I'm telling you it did.'

'Well if it did, how come I never heard about it?'

'That's it.' Hugh stood up, flung his hand out in a fascist salute. 'The Germans definitely deserve to win. Knowing all that about here? And us not knowing? And we living here all our lives?' He paused then broke into 'Deutschland, Deutschland über alles ...'

'Sit down, would you and try and pretend to be sane.' Matt smiled as he spoke. 'It's strange though. I mean, how come we never heard about it?'

'Your father didn't want you brought up looking backwards. No more than I did myself.'

Mention of their father always brought the same kind of quiet; a short, silence, a breath they all held for an instant as if retracing their steps to discover where he'd emerged from.

*

Mid morning, a few days after Christmas, Matt was upstairs sorting through papers and books when Hugh called up from the hall.

'There's a letter for you. From England. It's been opened by the censors.'

Matt flew down the stairs, snapped the letter from Hugh who was examining the sticker fixed to it in the censorship office.

Hugh stood waiting for Matt to open it, mystified when he put it directly into his pocket.

'What is it? Who is it from?'

Will, alerted by Hugh's interest in the letter, came to the top of the stairs.

'It's from no one.'

'A letter from no one?' Hugh scoffed, irritated by how covert Matt was being about it. He'd never known him to insist on privacy in this way.

'It's from his Scotland Yard contact.' Hugh shouted up at Will. 'Someone who can't be n-a-m-e-d.'

'For God's sake. It's from someone I met in Rathisland, an evacuee who's staying with her aunts and her uncle outside the town.'

'Woooooo …' A noise Hugh prolonged for several seconds, holding both hands up and backing off dramatically. 'I declare the man is smitten.'

'Would you ever shag off.' Matt went back upstairs, banged the door shut.

Downstairs, Hugh crooned Sinatra's 'Night and Day', virtually shouting the second verse: 'Night and day, you are the one / Only you beneath the moon or under the sun …'

Matt sat on the edge of his bed, holding up the envelope, turning it this way and that before opening it.

Written on the day Madelene arrived in London, it began with an account of her boat journey. She raced from one sensation to the next, delighted at being so much in the swing of things. There was a dance band on board, the Hal Hunter Orchestra, 'with lots and lots of couples dancing, men and women who after a while changed into uniform'. She gave over a full page to describing their dancing, 'quick steps and rumbas that had them gasping as they lurched for their chairs once the dance ended'. Matt assumed these were Irish serving members of the British forces returning to military duties, free, once they were out of Irish territorial waters, to reveal what they were about. Of course they could, he thought as he reread the letter, be British, or indeed other allied army personnel, returning after leave spent in Ireland. Whoever they were, Madelene was fascinated by them. If only you could have been there to see it for yourself, she wrote two, three times, each time punctuating that wish with an exclamation mark, an invitation to dance the night away in the smoky anonymity of that floating, in-between world.

Matt spent the whole afternoon writing back. He began by projecting ahead to spring, promising that the inchoate life it held was going to transform the universe, suffuse the Castle Wall Road with colours and scents as yet unknown, turn the lank, windswept, landscape into a lush, verdant paradise in which they would loll away whole afternoons: It was as lyrical as he could make it, an attempt to compete with the excitement that filled her letter. But Rathisland, he clearly saw when he reread what he'd written, appeared all the worse for being dressed up in words like 'inchoate', 'suffuse' and 'verdant.' It could never compete with the Hal Hunter Orchestra. He crumpled it up, stuffed it in his pocket, started again. 'It was great to get yours of the 19th though it didn't get here until today. It was opened by the censors who you probably had leaping around the office doing rumbas and quicksteps after the description you gave of the dance ...'

Telling her that the censors had opened her letter was a mistake, or so Matt decided when, a few days later, he received a reply. She did not understand that most letters coming from abroad were vetted and so was very put out to learn that some snoop, as she put it, had pored over everything she wrote. There was a kind of formal informality about her reply, a friendly but unsettling distance. It was as if she'd become her own censor. Whole pages read as if written by someone he didn't know very well, an English pen pal outlining how caught up everyone was in the war effort. Matt scrutinized those pages, homing in on words and phrases that brought her voice to life, breathing warmth into tepid references, magnifying whatever glints of affection he could find.

Back in Rathisland for the new term, he kept those letters in the inside pocket of his jacket, slipping his hand in to touch them several times every day, hardly able to wait until Madelene returned at the end of the month. Against the backdrop of that longing, Rathisland seemed greyer, more lifeless than ever. Looking out on the Square from his bedroom window, as he often found himself doing in the darkening afternoons, he sometimes imagined everything grinding to a halt. People going about their everyday business would begin to slow down, coming to a total standstill as though paralyzed by some silent, unseen force. And so it would remain, a still life of itself, its scarce, muted colours fading as darkness encroached.

And it was cold, insidiously cold in that drizzly, January way. Whenever he could he went for a walk out the Castle Wall Road, often welcoming the bite of raw, searing wind, the stoicism it demanded echoing his sense of enduring the days until Madelene returned. Sometimes, on those walks, he would dally at the top of Colls' lane. On one occasion he actually went down, no reason to call, just something he ended up doing without giving it any thought. The door-knocker, like a switch or button on a child's toy, set the house in motion. He no longer wanted to be there. Footsteps clacked up and down the stairs, doors creaked open and closed, voices whispered urgently to each other. He considered running away. But it was too late. Statia and Rose answered the door together, Statia to the fore, her head thrown back theatrically as though first in a long receiving line.

'Mr Duggan,' she said with a mix of shock and surprise. 'It's Mr Duggan.' She turned to Rose, said it again. 'It's Mr Duggan.'

They peered at him for a moment or two then both speaking at once asked him to come in.

'No. No, thanks. I was just passing by and thought I'd come down and ask when Madelene is coming back.' It was a question to which he knew the answer all too well, but never the less, found it reassuring to hear them say Sunday week.

A few days before she was due to arrive, walking along the Castle Wall Road, he imagined he saw her walking towards him, a mirage forming and reforming in sweeps of sudden, flinty rain. He slowed down, forced himself to abandon the line of thought that had created that illusion, determined to regain the run of himself. And still the figure kept coming, its outline no longer indistinct. He stopped, reluctant to abandon his disbelief, all the while preparing for the moment when she, Madelene, now running towards him, would disappear back into the flurry of rain from which she'd emerged. And he continued to prepare for that moment, unable to abandon his disbelief even as she tumbled into his open arms. He drew back, looked into her face, touched the wisps of her hair curling at the sodden rim of her cloche hat, gripped her shoulders, shook her until whatever doubt remained about her being there had vanished.

'You're back?' He cupped his hands around her cheeks. 'I mean you are back, aren't you?'

'I think so.' She laughed. Pressed in close to him, shuddering a little, heaving breath unevenly.

'You're crying. You've been crying.' He drew back and looked into her eyes, now certain she'd been crying.

'No. it's the rain. See.' She pointed to the droplets of rain streaming down her flushed cheeks. But her eyes, Matt saw, were full of tears.

'What happened?'

'I'm so relieved to be here. That's all.' She began to sob, shuddering as she tried to draw breath between sobs, abandoning herself to the ever tightening embrace in which Matt held her.

'What can have you this upset?' He loosened his grip, drew back and looked at her again. She turned her head, then heaving breath, blurted; 'I don't want to go into it.'

Matt didn't know what to say. He enfolded her in his arms, trying, by drawing her as close as possible, to contain her convulsive shaking. Several minutes passed before it began to ebb and even longer before she started to breath evenly.

'What is it? Please Madelene. Surely you can tell me?'

'Lots of things.' Madelene swallowed in an attempt to steady the tremor in her voice. 'Lots of things. There were rows. Dad got called back, which is why I came early. And Mum … oh it's a bit of a long story.'

They began to walk.

'I'm listening.'

Madelene said nothing for a few seconds, then cleared her throat. 'Not now, some other time. I'm here. Look.' She pointed at herself, then reached up, gripped the back of his neck, turned his head towards her and laughing, through her tears, said, 'See, It's me. Can we go to the cinema? That's what we'll do. We'll go to the cinema. It's nearly five. It'll open at half seven.'

'Well. I suppose …' Matt paused.

'No.' Madelene said. 'Two and a half hours. That's too long. No we won't go. It's just that it's so cold. So wet. And I really don't want to be with Rose and Statia. Not now, anyway.'

Matt came to a standstill as he recalled the wide-eyed way Rose and Statia had said *Mr Duggan* when they answered the door the other evening.

'I'll tell you what. We'll go back, slip down that path by the side of the orchard and go into the barn, where it's not cold or wet.'

'But if we're seen?'

'We'll just make sure we're not.'

Ducking down behind the wall leading to the chicken run, Matt practically on his hands and knees, they scampered towards the barn, deciding, in an urgently whispered exchange, that they'd go singly across the open ground at the far end of the chicken run.

'You first,' Matt said, raising his head from his crouched position and pointing in the direction of the barn. 'Go on.'

Madelene tore off, her head bowed until she reached it.

Inside, the smell of hay, of warmer weather, of different climes, a place dark and apart, all contributed to the urgency with which they slumped onto the hay. They hardly spoke during the hour or so they spent there, just clung together as though holding out against some great force. And there were new intimacies, venial explorations that transported them to places where fear and pleasure clashed; pleasure invariably reined back by fear.

'I better go or they'll have a search party out.'

'We can come another time,' Matt smiled, 'Better get rid of the evidence.' He began to pick bits of hay off Madelene's cardigan.

And back they did come, time and time again in the weeks that followed. So much so that a routine emerged: Setting out for a walk, just as they'd done throughout the previous autumn, they'd head up the lane towards the Castle Wall Road. Once they'd turned the corner, they'd sneak back on the field side of the hedge, duck down behind the wall, the Maginot line as they came to call it, shoot past the chicken run, El Alamein, then out onto the open ground, the Sudetenland, the barn, Honolulu, now only seconds away. Each breathless arrival was an achievement, a triumphant entry into a world that had all but replaced any other to which they'd ever belonged.

It was a world in which they remained, even when there were other people around. If in or about the town together they would play at being undercover agents operating within enemy territory, whispering to each other as they walked down Main Street: 'Avoid the post office. Everything is reported'; 'Don't look up, just act as though we're not together, Mrs Healy is watching from her upstairs window'; 'Don't ask questions and say nothing, absolutely nothing about Honolulu.' It was a game into which all of Rathisland unwittingly entered, such was the level of surveillance of everyone by everyone else.

Even the young children could be seen to participate, a point that struck home on the one and only time Matt and Madelene did go to the cinema. The three-penny front seats, reserved for children, were full. Matt recognized at least a dozen pupils from his own classes. Several of them spent the evening kneeling on their seats, their backs to the screen, staring directly up at him and Madelene. They only turned to look at the film, *The Texas Rangers Ride Again*, if there was gunfire or a saloon bar smash-up. At one point Madelene gestured to them to turn around. Most shrank away, but two, who thought she'd waved at them, waved back and continued to wave on and off for the remainder of the film.

All that spring Dixie had been working on a steam-powered engine fuelled by turf. This gizmo, a gangly amalgam of crudely welded iron rods, oil-coated pulley wheels and taut steel wire was housed in one of the long line of open sheds to the left of the house. It was something of a curiosity, attracting people from far and wide. Men, sometimes accompanied by their wives and children all dressed up for the occasion, would arrive in the yard, usually in the early evening or on Sunday afternoons. Dixie never tired of getting the engine going. He'd light and stoke the burner, chatting and answering questions while the steam built up, then look on with a kind of befuddled pride when the pistons began to rise and fall. Long, detailed conversations would often follow, with the visitors puzzling over the problems, gingerly presented by Dixie, of adapting the engine for use in a locomotive. His head would remain bowed as he listened to their proposals, always waiting until they'd fully had their say. He'd then repeat those proposals as though he hadn't already spotted all the reasons why they wouldn't work, mull over them, looking this way and that at the engine, delaying the moment when he would reluctantly reveal the flaw in their suggestion. Statia and Rose, delighted with the steady flow of visitors to the yard, would stand a few paces back form the demonstration, two exotic birds, a maternal smugness in their stance that was strikingly at odds with their burlesque finery.

A few glorious days, sprightly advance scouts at the beginning of May, marked the arrival of summer. Children, hopscotching and skipping, led a sort of victory parade down Main Street, all the while calling noisily to each other, shaking the rest of Rathisland out of the deep, lifeless slumber from which it was slowly beginning to emerge. Mrs Sheridan, more by way of celebration than necessity, covered the front door with a sunscreen, a coarse blue-and-yellow, striped cotton drape with neatly tailored openings for the letter-box, the handle, the knocker and the lock. Both windows of Tony Lehane's drapery shop were hung from top to bottom with orangey-yellow cellophane to protect the garments on display from the fading effects of direct sunlight. People no longer scurried to and fro, finding time instead to linger and chat. The school day began by flinging open all the windows, creating a fresh, roomy aura inside, a welcome contrast to the cloying atmosphere that had pervaded all winter.

Chapter 12

From the beginning of June onwards, with only a few weeks to go to the long summer holidays, things began to loosen up in school. Matt welcomed the lax atmosphere, longer mid-morning breaks, fewer lightening-strike visits from Carmody, less work to correct. This was increasingly the run of things as the June flitted by, so it struck Matt as curious, when on the last Monday in the month, there was an unmistakably furtive atmosphere in the classroom; covert, urgent whispering whenever he turned to write anything on the board; silence when he swung back to see what was going on. On one of those fast swivels, designed to catch, name and warn someone, he spotted a black leather glove on the floor of the aisle directly in front of where he was standing. The atmosphere tightened as he stepped forward to pick it up.

'*Cé leis é?*' He waited, expecting someone to lay claim to it.

'The Germans. It's from one of the German planes that's after landing in Baunaughra.' The pupil who spoke,

Alphonsus Conroy, turned around, looking for support, which Pádraig Costigan was quick to offer.

'Yeah. They'll all be here in …' Stark-eyed, he searched for a way of describing how fast they were heading for the town, 'here in …,' he looked about, 'here in a … with guns that can kill a hundred people in a minute.' He demonstrated the size of the guns, stretching his arms out as far as they would go. Soon the whole class was swapping information about the supposed invasion. A few stood up to look out the windows, their faces brimming with hope of finding the invaders there. Matt banged the desk with the back of the blackboard duster, creating enough quiet to ensure that the second, louder bang would bring silence.

'That's enough.' He left the glove down.' Whoever owns this glove may collect it at the end of school. Now, down to work.'

The pupils opened their books in a desultory way, several of them glancing up at Matt, trying to gauge the chances of raising the question of the invasion again. But Matt wasn't having any of it. The story had emerged against a backdrop of several false alarms, a whole winter of smoke without fire, a long litany of impossible and outlandish happenings, among them the citing of a flock of low-flying geese, each with explosives strapped to its underbelly, all dreamed up on the grey, unchanging streets of Rathisland.

He returned to the blackboard and continued where he'd left off, waiting for things to settle. When they did, he picked up the glove and began to examine it. A fresh bout of whispering forced him to drop it, but not before he saw that it was, in fact, German made. However, he didn't regard that as particularly significant. There were lots of similar, so-called souvenirs in circulation. He showed it to Carmody and Canning at lunchtime, told them jokingly about the supposed Baunaughra landing. Carmody tried it on, marvelling at the workmanship, flexing his fingers in the fleecy lining while he held forth about German know-how, German superiority and the prospect of a German victory, which he said would give England a dose of its own medicine. 'And not before it's time, either,' he added, drawing his lips resolutely together. It was the sort of quip that in the normal course of events might have triggered a chuckle of agreement from Canning or Matt. But there and then, in the crisis of loyalties thrown up by the war, it was met by a kind of befuddled silence. Without warning, Carmody guffawed loudly. It was an invitation to Canning and Matt to make light of what he had said, which they did by guffawing loudly too.

The arrival of two Irish Army vehicles into Rathisland just after lunch came as a surprise; a surprise to Matt, but not to the pupils. He heard Canning's classes, second and third, scramble down the corridor, and from the window of his classroom watched them tear across the playground, leaping like gazelles across the plains, heading for the roadside to greet the arriving convoy. Matt assumed Canning had given them the go-ahead, having decided it was one of those occasions when rules could be set aside. As he discovered, though not until after he'd given his own classes the go-ahead to join them, they'd mutinied. With Canning's and Matt's own classes now gathered at the roadside, Carmody was under considerable pressure to allow his classes out. If he had taken a firm stance, stood in front of them, brandishing the bamboo cane he used so frequently, he could have kept them there, but he himself was curious. More than curious, he was determined that if the war had come to Rathisland, as appeared to be the case, he was not going to miss out on the action. His classes joined the throng.

The convoy, a jeep and an armoured car on its way to investigate the supposed Luftwaffe landing on Baunaughra Bog, was cheered on by well over seventy pupils, offering every variety of salute, including tensely outstretched arms accompanied by roars of *Heil Hitler*. Matt stood beside Canning, listening sympathetically as he whispered details of his pupils' mutiny, certain that Carmody, twisting his way towards them through the cheering pupils, was, at the very least, going to demand an explanation.

'Might as well let them follow on at this stage.' Carmody spoke from the distance, indicating to the army of incredulous young faces that they had permission to follow the convoy. Matt and Canning looked at each other in astonishment, both registering the notion that there had to be a catch. It occurred to Matt that it could be a form of punishment, a way of impressing on Canning and himself the folly of allowing the pupils out in the first place. But it wasn't, as they plainly saw on the two-mile hike to Baunaughra Bog, with Carmody lagging a bit behind them all the way, his hopes for a German foothold on Irish soil periodically released in short swear-like gasps.

'I could think of worse.' Canning looked at Matt, anticipating he might think differently about the Germans now that they had arrived.

'There's always worse,' Matt replied.

Ahead, the pupils, like the children of Hamlyn following the Pied Piper, kept pace with the armoured car and the jeep, two or three panting along behind in the ever-increasing distance between them and the advancing convoy.

Whatever disappointment there was about the absence of a fleet of sleek Luftwaffe bombers on Baunaughra Bog was readily offset by the sight of a brownish, oddly shaped plane, precariously balanced on the edge of a steep cutting ridge, its nose dipping forward into the pool of luminous water below, its raised double-finned-tail, stark and angular against the enormous June sky. 'A Stuka, it's a Stuka,' one pupil announced, soon to be corrected by the class authority, Kevin Dwyer, who declared it to be a Messerschmitt Bf110 G-4. Anyway, there it was, real and unreal by turns, tangible proof of a war, which, by and large, had reached Rathisland only in carefully measured phrases, shortages and inconveniences of one sort or another.

The soldiers were bunched around their commanding officer, who pointed this way and that before circling the air decisively with his index finger. They stamped out their cigarettes and began sealing off the site, then, joking and laughing, slung ropes to each other as though they'd been through it all before. The pupils watched their every move, their heads rising and falling as they followed the arc of the wooden mallets used to sink the cordoning rods. Every now and then they hurriedly turned to each other, a few seconds snatched from the action, to predict what was going to happen next.

Carmody cleared his throat to speak to the officer, repositioning a fallen cordoning rod in a tuft of sedge close to where he was standing with Matt and Canning.

'Looks like the crew bailed out before she came down.' Carmody's eyes narrowed in judgment. When the officer didn't reply he tilted his head to one side, exaggeratedly going through the motions of working out how the pilots, or the pilot and the gunner as the pupils had already informed him, might have parachuted out.

'Great weather,' the officer, a sunken-jawed man with a tightly rippled brow, said briskly, making it clear he was not going to be drawn into speculation about the fate of the airmen, even though he must, it struck Matt later, have known that one of them, the gunner, had bailed out some ten miles to the north and was already in custody.

'You may be sure they won't be as tight-lipped when they're passing the details onto His Majesty's Government,' Carmody muttered under his breath as the officer went on to check the next cordoning post.

'A bit on the official side, alright.' Words Canning pitched into the uneasy silence that followed.

Matt was on the brink of pointing out that the officer was just doing his job, that he had to follow the protocol demanded by neutrality, but held back when it struck him that Carmody would see it as pro-British and therefore unpatriotic.

Although the soldiers continued to refuse to be drawn into any discussion about the Messerschmitt, fresh information about it somehow kept filtering through the crowd; information, Matt began to think, the pupils must have had before they arrived in school. In this way, it emerged that the crash, or the forced landing as it would subsequently be referred to, had remained unreported for several hours, during which time it was completely looted. Even some of the instruments, fixtures on the dashboard, had been hacked off.

In the course of the investigation that followed, a few things, including an unopened packet of cigarettes and some mildly pornographic postcards, were recovered. Sergeant Cotton, charged with investigating the looting, made an attempt to establish who had brought the glove to school, but Carmody was less than cooperative.

'You never know where all the stuff they get will end up,' he warned, when Matt went to collect the roll books the morning Sergeant Cotton had arranged to visit the school. 'Some say it's passed on to the British. And I wouldn't be a bit surprised, with the way that crowd above in Dublin have turned on their own.'

Later that morning Carmody arrived into Matt's classroom, accompanied by the sergeant and stood there, arms folded, scowling more fiercely than Matt had ever seen him scowl before. No one dared look up, let alone speak. The sergeant, a blocky, slow-moving man, seemed equally intimidated by Carmody, so it fell to Matt to ask who had brought the glove into school. When, after a very short time no one had owned up, Carmody turned to the sergeant.

'You're only wasting your time here.'

The sergeant looked around the classroom for a bit, then, escorted by Carmody, lumbered over to the door and left. Within seconds, Pádraig Costigan's hand was up.

'It's the pilot's glove. And if he's caught he'll be brought to the North and handed to the English who'll give him electric shocks until he says everything he knows.'

Slack jawed and open mouthed, the other pupils listened.

'That's enough of that *raiméis*,' Matt said. But spurred on by the gaping fascination of the others, Pádraig stood up. 'And when they're done with him they'll give him a killer shock and then throw him in a ditch.'

'*Suí síos*,' Matt demanded, trying to decide what to do if he persisted. He slid slowly into his seat, at which point Matt decided to calm things down by giving dictation.

Every day there were new suppositions about the Messerschmitt's mission, about the other planes that had reputedly accompanied it, about the fate of the wreck. As well as that, there were a number of sightings or possible sightings of the missing crewman: a figure spotted at dusk at the edge of Balladerry wood; his footsteps found on the path that ran along a stretch of the stream behind the town; remains of a fire he'd supposedly lit discovered up near Knockfinn

Quarry. The investigation into his whereabouts, spear-headed by a detective from Dublin, followed up some of these reports in a low-key, routine way.

The first report with a definite ring of truth to it didn't surface until almost a week after the landing. Dr Corrigan, a regular at Mrs Sheridan's card evenings, was the source. A colleague of his, Dr White, a GP in a town seven miles or so from Rathisland, was called to a remote farmhouse early on the morning of the landing to treat a young uniformed German with a dislocated shoulder. What followed emerged as though from a slow dripping tap, because Dr Corrigan, too tedious to engage attention under normal circumstances, was determined to make the most of the interest his story generated. Lips pursed judiciously he explained that his colleague, Dr White, tried to find out how the injury happened, but the man appeared to speak no English and was in considerable pain. As soon as the dislocated shoulder was set, Dr White, anxious to get back for morning surgery, undertook to inform the gardaí, assuring the widow that they would come and take the injured man into custody. But late for surgery and faced with a number of patients in immediate need of care, Dr White didn't inform the gardaí until midday. When they got to the farmhouse the pilot was no longer there. The widow, fearful of the attention she knew the incident would draw to her, readily agreed to the gardaí's request not to speak about it until the investigation was complete. Dr White also agreed to this request, but nonetheless told Dr Corrigan, in confidence, as he, Dr Corrigan, repeatedly emphasized to the six people in Mrs Sheridan's drawing room.

Matt could hardly wait to tell Madelene, who all week had talked non-stop about the pilot. 'What will happen if he gets caught?' she'd asked Matt as soon as she heard the news, not at all convinced when he said, 'Nothing.'

'Nothing, nothing at all?'; words she plied with disbelief, prompting him to explain that he would be brought by the gardaí to the Curragh Camp where, together with other Germans captured on Irish soil, he'd be looked after until the war ended.

'What if he thinks he's in England and hides?' she'd asked, leaping ahead before Matt could reply, to outline a worse fate; the possibility that he could be injured, dying slowly in some field around here, as she put it.

With these and Madelene's many other ongoing concerns for the pilot in mind, Matt rushed along the Castle Wall Road the following evening, delighted to be bringing news of him to her. Quickstepping his way down the lane, Matt saw Dixie standing gormlessly in the middle of the yard, no indication of which direction he'd come from, or which direction he was headed.

'Great evening,' Matt said with all the bonhomie he'd come to address Dixie, unperturbed when Dixie just continued to stare at him.

'If you had a few minutes?' Dixie muttered as Matt brushed by, 'Costigan came,' he tilted his head very slightly towards the outhouse.

Thinking only about the impact that news of the pilot was going to have on Madelene, Matt did not reply. Instead he glanced impatiently at the outhouse, expecting Dixie to realize he didn't want to be waylaid. But Dixie just stood there in his oily overalls, now embarrassed at having asked Matt to do something he clearly didn't want to do, but not, it soon became apparent, going to backtrack. Matt wondered if he expected him to challenge Costigan as he'd done the previous September, something he didn't have the will, interest or even inclination to do. He'd come to regard Costigan as an out-and-out chancer, a man whose antics and schemes Rathisland tolerated because of the part his father had played in the War of Independence.

'If he just saw that you were around.' Dixie cast his eyes down, an aura of helplessness about him that Matt was unable to ignore.

'Alright, but it'll only be for a few minutes.'

Matt's annoyance on seeing Costigan rapidly turned to anger when, affecting disgust, Costigan said: 'What the fuck are you doing here?'

Matt resisted the urge to tell Costigan he was about to ask him the same question, distracted, in that same moment, by a figure standing behind Costigan, partly concealed by his bulk and further obscured by the lack of light. Peering into the darkness Matt saw a man of his own age, less tall and with a shock of fair curly hair. He was shifting about a bit, trying to move forward but unable to do so because Costigan, squared up as if trying to conceal him, was in his way. Eventually he stepped over the oil drums on Costigan's left, springing forward with his right arm outstretched. As soon as Matt saw that his other arm was in a sling he realized he was the missing pilot.

Of all the people to fall in with. A stroke of real bad luck, Matt thought. He tried to figure out how it could have happened, diverted by the image of Pádraig Costigan shooting up like a jack-in-the-box after Sergeant Cotton had left the classroom, telling everyone that if the pilot was caught he'd be handed over to the British who would electrocute him and throw him into a ditch. Disastrous, Matt thought, if that's what the pilot has been told by Costigan.

Now standing directly in front of Matt, the pilot reached out and shook hands. 'Josef,' he said resolutely, squeezing Matt's hand until the middle knuckles grated. He repeated his name, adding a German surname.

To their right, closely observed by Costigan, Dixie busied himself with the radio. Stations came and went in muffled snatches, languages merging into each other, forming a sound whorl into which a myriad of voices disappeared. Dixie glanced up at Costigan. He'd located and was now fine-tuning the station he'd been tracking. The signal was weak. 'Shush …' Costigan demanded, though no one was making a sound. Josef started to laugh quietly to himself, amused, it seemed, by the seriousness with which Costigan was approaching the radio programme. Costigan snuffled loudly, making no secret of his irritation when Josef began humming in accompaniment to the song that followed, 'It's Springtime in County Clare'. Observing how frustrated Costigan was by this, Matt began to hum too. When the song ended, a woman, introduced as Frau Schneider, read out some recipes, one of which was for some sort of cabbage dish.

'Useful, very useful,' Josef laughed loudly, joined by Matt when Frau Schneider began to describe, in a near ecstatic state, different ways of crushing walnuts. The possibility of steering things back onto a serious track, fast fading by the second, was dealt a final blow when the next item, 'Darkie Music and Fairy Tales by Uncle Remus', was announced.

'I don't think so, the *Abwehr*,' Josef said, pronouncing each word carefully, allowing the full extent of his scepticism to surface. He looked quizzically at Costigan, who Matt surmised, must have brought him along in the belief that the broadcast would be directly from the *Abwehr*.

'Bide your time.' Costigan stared threateningly at the radio.

'This is good. Good music.' Josef nodded rhythmically, clicking his fingers to the jazzy piano tune belting unevenly out of the exposed speaker. Just then the station blanked out. No warning. No weakening of the signal. It just stopped.

Dixie struggled to relocate it but only succeeded in getting a high-pitched, piercing noise. Costigan crouched over him, urging him to continue, but every time Dixie approached the point on the dial where he expected to locate the station, the same loud, piercing noise sounded again.

'Some fucker has put the kibosh on it.' Costigan straightened up, resigned in a reproachful, querulous sort of way to the notion that the broadcast had been sabotaged. Matt wasn't sure if the keen interest Josef took in this claim was ironic or not. Either way it was short-lived, because as Matt went to leave Josef switched all his attention to him, holding out his hand and smiling in an open, trusting way.

Across the yard, Madelene was sitting on the front-door step, her hands clasped around her knees, the tips of her sandals peeping out from beneath the hem of her wide-skirted summer frock.

'I saw you going in.' She stood up, brushed the back of her frock with a sweep of her hands.

'So you know who's in there with Costigan?' Matt raised his eyebrows a little and smiled.

'They just arrived before you, asked where Dixie was. He's completely different looking than I thought.'

The outhouse door opened. Costigan, followed jauntily by Josef, sloped out and headed for the lane. As they turned onto it, Josef spotted Madelene and Matt. He stopped, waved and seemed to be about to go over when Costigan, already a few paces ahead, turned around and said something to him. Matt and Madelene, both smiling, waved slowly, then followed Josef's progress up the lane.

'How in Christ's name did the poor devil fall into Costigan's hands?' Matt's said as Josef disappeared around the bend.

'He is going to … Costigan is bringing someone here at first light, who's going to …'

'Coming here?' Matt cut in, eyes popping in disbelief.

'Yes. Dixie said he could stay in the barn tonight.' She pointed to the entrance leading to the farmyard.

'Agreed with who? Costigan I suppose.' Words Matt plied with a mix of concern and derision.

'Someone …' Madelene hesitated, less sure of herself now, 'Someone's coming who's bringing him to Donegal where a fishing boat will take him to somewhere he can get to Norway from.'

'Costigan told you that?'

'No. He told Dixie, who told Rose and Statia.'

'Does Dixie have any idea of the danger of it, the trouble he'll get into if he's found out? Probably everyone else as well?'

Madelene, flustered by the anger with which Matt spoke, shrugged her shoulders.

'It's a stupid plan. And Dixie is a fool.'

Madelene braced herself to reply. 'Just think what it must be like being in a country you don't know, trying to talk to people in a language that isn't your own, with them trying to catch you to put you in a prison …' Her voice began to tremble.

'For God sake, he's German,' Matt said forcibly, 'Are you a fool too? He's the enemy; your enemy. He could have been on a mission to bomb places you know. Your parents even.'

'It's nothing to do with that now,' she said, her voice breaking a little before she continued, 'He's here and …' She drew breath, cleared her throat in an attempt to steady her voice, but it was too late. 'I hate it. I hate it all. I want to be at home. I want to be back with my Mum and Dad even if they're being bombed,' words that were all but drowned out by a convulsive rush of tears.

Matt put his arm around her, no inkling that her tears

could have been prompted by anything other that the scorn he'd poured on the case she was making for Josef.

'The good part of it is …', he began in an attempt to recoup. 'The good part of it is that he's staying in the barn.'

With tears continuing to stream down her cheeks, Madelene looked up at him, her expression blank and uncomprehending.

'He *is* staying in the barn. Isn't he?' Matt spoke slowly, trying to pick up the thread of their conversation. Madelene's expression didn't change.

'It means if he's caught,' he raised his index finger as he might have done in the classroom,' Dixie won't get in trouble. He can just deny that he knew anything about it.'

Madelene continued to look at him uncomprehendingly.

'That's the good part, him being in the barn.' Matt said again.

After a moment or two Madelene nodded in a resigned sort of way, drew a deep breath and said, 'Sorry. I don't know what came over me.'

'Nothing a walk won't cure. Come on.' He gripped her upper arm, directing her towards the lane.

'Matt, I think I'm going to have to lie down.' She placed the palm of her hand on her forehead, resting it there for a bit, before smoothing her hair back with it. 'Tomorrow. when this is all over.' She wiped her cheek with the back of her hand. 'I feel so stupid, just bursting out crying like that.' Then almost in the same breath, 'Oh no, not tomorrow. I forgot. Tomorrow evening I'm bringing the aunts to visit Mrs Young. Her husband died a few weeks ago.' She pulled a face, smiled, wiped her cheek with the back of her hand.

'They're well able to manage by themselves,' Matt said, long since convinced that Rose and Statia pretended to be unable to drive the trap so as to keep Madelene with them.

'You can play cards with Hilda,' she laughed, pursing her lips to make Mrs Sheridan's name sound pretentious.

'Saturday after lunch. OK?'

The front door, which always had to be forced at a particular point, began to open behind them. 'It's usually not this bad in dry weather,' Rose said, rattling the door until the knocker sounded.

'I'll walk over with you. I don't want them seeing me like this.' Madelene ushered Matt away from the step and towards the bottom of the lane, Rose and Statia's voices rising behind them, each fussily instructing the other on how to open the door.

Spears of early evening sun shot through the chestnut trees as Matt walked along the Castle Wall Road, all the while thinking of the things he ought to have said when Madelene burst out crying: *What of it. Don't worry about it. You could do a lot worse than crying. What's stupid about crying. Here, come on,* he wraps his arms around her, *There's just us, just us and that's the whole world to me.*

Chapter 13

The next day was even warmer than the preceding few days, but there was a stillness to it that by the afternoon had begun to hang heavily, compressing the motionless heat to the point that even walking required effort.

All morning Matt had been mulling over the events of the previous evening. He stood staring out the window of his classroom hardly registering what he was looking at, wishing more than ever that he'd responded differently when Madelene had began to cry. By lunchtime, what he ought to have said had taken on a definite shape. Going over it again and again throughout the afternoon, he grew increasingly frustrated at having to wait until the following day to see her. As the pupils packed up to leave it struck him that he could go to Colls, there and then, wondering, as he thought it through, why it hadn't already occurred to him. She's not due to go off with her aunts until after supper, he thought. He surveyed his desk, two separate piles of copybooks, a large bottle of Quink ink, the chalk box held together with yellow Bisodol tape and a small stack of books; it could all be left as it was. He rushed over to the windows, hurriedly closed them and left.

When he arrived in Colls' yard, Dixie was demonstrating the turf-powered gizmo to two men. Standing in the shade cast by the great sycamore, Statia and Rose watched, Statia gripping Rose's arm as though the gizmo might take off at any moment. They bowed slightly at Matt from the distance, the same greeting as always, gracious, warm but tinged with mistrust, not perhaps mistrust of Matt, but of the world in general. Dixie, unused to seeing Matt in the mid afternoon, stopped, his face slackening like that of a staring child.

'Great day,' Matt said, slowing down as he approached Dixie, picking up pace as he brushed by, his mind firmly made up not to join in any discussion about Josef, in particular to avoid acknowledging that he knew the plans for his escape. It was over: Josef was well on his way to Donegal.

'She's not inside. She's not there. She's off walking this past hour.' Words Dixie slung at Matt with a quick twist of his head.

'I'll wait.' Matt said after a moment or two, knowing Madelene could not be gone for much longer. He lingered a bit in the middle of the yard then strolled over to the front-door steps, turned and was about to sit down when he saw Dixie coming from where Rose and Statia were standing, his lips slightly moving as he rehearsed whatever he was about to say.

'Powerful weather,' Matt smiled, drawing back a little as Dixie positioned himself uncomfortably close, about, it seemed, to say something confidential; something about Josef, Matt thought, bracing himself to resist joining in.

'Powerful day,' Dixie repeated, glaring at Matt, one eye

angled sharply to the fore. 'I was on the way to see what's up below in the stream field when these lads came.' He tilted his head in the direction of the two men but didn't take his sharply angled eye off Matt. 'One of the cows down below in the stream field hasn't stopped bawling all morning.' He spoke rapidly, moving from one foot to the other, now poised to continue but unable to bring the words to the surface. Familiar with Dixie's near inability to ask anything of anyone Matt tried to figure out what he was getting at. He wondered if he wanted him to go down and investigate. But Dixie had never involved him in anything to do with the farm. He knew nothing about it. He couldn't imagine how he could be of help, so he just waited, trying to anticipate where the conversation was leading, increasingly ill at ease while, inches away from his face, Dixie foraged awkwardly for words.

'Would you go down ...' he eventually blurted out, now turning and looking at Matt side-eyed.

'If Madelene comes back, you'll tell her where I am.'

'I'll do that.'

Matt headed off, familiar enough with Dixie's ways not to turn around when Dixie, as though releasing a backlog of jammed words, said, 'Some of the cows, some of the cows were separated from the calves only yesterday and what with the stream so low, one of them could've crossed into Hannigan's moor looking for her calf and ...' He stopped abruptly, then loudly added, 'and got stuck there.'

Matt knew the lie of the farm. When the weather was fine, Statia and Rose would wander into the fields after supper and in a slow, aimless way saunter in the direction of the stream, gathering bits of kindling as they went. Matt had seen them from the road a number of times in recent weeks, two daubs of colour, sometimes at a considerable distance apart, a tranquillity about their gait and pace that made them seem peculiarly at home with their surroundings. He'd never been beyond the field beside the house, the copse field as it was known, so as he made his way down towards the stream field he kept looking back, intrigued by how small, how turned-in-on-themselves the house and the outbuildings appeared.

He remained in the shade of the hedge, staying, for the most part, on the narrow, well-trodden sheep track running close to it. Now and then he stopped to listen for the stranded cow but heard nothing except thin, distant calling, light scraps of sound no sooner heard than they were scattered by other, closer sounds, a bird scurrying from the hedgerow or the nervous bleat of a sheep in the adjoining field.

Climbing over the ancient, wooden stile leading into the furze scrub at the top of the stream field, he heard that calling again, now more distinctly. It could, he thought, be an echo. It could be Madelene, returned from wherever she'd been, now calling from behind, trying to catch up, her voice travelling past him to some point beyond, the high ground at the far side of the stream maybe, then bouncing back to create the illusion that she was over there. He stood up on the rickety stile and manoeuvred himself around, peering back through the powdery haze of dandelion down lying low over the fields, back towards the house. He heard her voice again, much clearer now, coming, not from the direction in which he was looking, but from the stream field. He tore through the furze bushes.

She must have spotted the distressed animal and was trying to help it, he thought, brushing the last of the furze bushes aside, all set to surprise her.

As he stepped into the open field, all his facial and neck muscles suddenly tightened, making it impossible to turn his head that fraction to the left necessary to see what he had, in fact, already glimpsed but could not bring himself to look at again; Madelene skipping along beside Josef, their shoulders brushing carelessly against each other, her laughter loud, almost taunting as she side-stepped away from him, then swung in right beside him as he put his arm around her waist. Matt edged back into the furze thicket, only able to see their heads now, his temples throbbing, his mouth caked dry, chest tightened to the point that he could only breath in short, sharp snatches.

He looked around as he might in a pitch-dark, unfamiliar place, trying to find his bearings, blind even to the movement of his own limbs. He didn't work through the details of what he had, at some gut level, already decided to do. He was afraid to consider it, afraid he'd discover some overwhelming reason why he shouldn't do it. And with that he left, breaking into a trot as soon as he was out of the furze thicket. He moved rapidly along the sheep track, inhaling the scent of the dying hawthorn blossom, its sickly sweetness imprinting itself indelibly as a noxious, poisonous odour. To avoid Dixie, Rose and Statia, he cut across the fields to the road, then headed for the town, not slowing for an instant, even when back in the house, he asked Mrs Sheridan if he could borrow Evelyn's bike. 'Just for a cycle,' he said, quickstepping it to the shed, soon cycling furiously to the garda barracks in Abbeyleix.

Spurred on by what he was too angry, too distressed even to name, he just pedalled; pedalled with every ounce of his strength, all his thoughts centred on Josef's capture.

There was, despite the warm weather, a fire smouldering in the grate of the small, almost miniature, cast-iron fireplace of the cramped garda barracks office. Matt stood facing it as he waited for someone to appear, fixing on the array of official forms and leaflets on the narrow mantel ledge, desperate to focus on anything other than what had brought him there. But even the random thoughts triggered by those forms and leaflets had a feverish edge. Everything in the room seemed like an exaggerated version of itself, hostile, threatening, loud.

The sergeant's wife, wearing an apron with fluted lapels drooping limply onto her bare upper arms, appeared at the door leading to their living quarters. The little office filled with the fumes of frying lard.

'He'll be with you in a minute.' She stood in the doorway, her long face tilted to examine Matt. She remained at the door, staring unselfconsciously, moving only a fraction as the sergeant brushed by.

'Well, what can we do for you?' the sergeant asked in a self-satisfied sort of way, drawing his chin in as if to swallow or suppress a belch. He was abnormally tall, six-feet-six, maybe more. His collar stud was unfastened and his loosened tie, bunching out a little, was speckled with crumbs. He stretched his arm back and eased the door shut, gently backing his wife into the kitchen.

'I have something to report.'

'You have? Well you've come to the right place at any rate.' He grinned, making light of the gravity with which Matt had spoken.

'It's about the German pilot. I know where he is.' Words Matt rushed at the sergeant, expecting his composure would change, which it didn't. He just turned around, calmly took a wad of cream-coloured paper from the shelf behind, slipped a pen out from the corner of his jacket pocket and slowly twisted the top off, looking at it as though he wasn't quite sure if he was going about it correctly.

'Fire ahead. We'll take your name first.'

He wrote down Matt's name, then his address, stood back a little, drew in his chin and narrowed his eyes as he looked over what he'd written. Then, as though he'd only just registered that Matt didn't live in Abbeyleix, said, 'What brought you here? Why didn't you go to the barracks in Rathisland?'

'If I was seen, it would get around that I ...' He stopped abruptly, began again. 'If I was seen, it would get around and the pilot could be alerted.' The sergeant leaned forward, rested one elbow on the counter.

'And your position, Mr Duggan?' He glanced officiously at the top of the page as if to confirm that he'd got Matt's name right.

'Teacher. In the school in Rathisland. He's sleeping in a shed, Colls' shed, just outside the town. They know nothing about him. I saw him going in there.'

The sergeant stood back, gestured to Matt with an open hand to stop, which he did, relieved all the same, to have said that much.

'The best thing is if we start off at the beginning. When did you see this man?'

'About two hours ago.'

He looked at his watch. 'Four. I'll put down four o'clock. And tell us, what made you think he was the German pilot?'

The question dangled precariously between them for a moment as Matt anxiously searched for a reply, swallowing hard before he said, 'By the look of him. And I'd heard that he'd dislocated his shoulder. His arm was in a sling.' He wedged his finger in between the rim of his collar and his neck, momentarily distracted by the clamminess of his skin.

'And that was the first time you saw this man?'

He nooded, wondering if the sergeant was leading him into some kind of trap.

'The next thing we need to know is how long you saw him for and …' he paused as though he'd forgotten his lines and was waiting to be prompted, 'And how clearly you saw him.'

How, Matt wondered, could he remain so unmoved. The investigation into the whereabouts of the pilot was still going on. The detective sent from Dublin had stayed in Dowlings' Hotel for most of the previous week. Lots of people had been questioned. Fearful that he wouldn't take action straight away, or might not take action at all, he told the sergeant that Colls' barn wasn't the sort of place a man on the run would stay for very long. 'Too much coming and going to the yard,' he added, observing the sergeant closely, hoping for a sign, a change in his expression, something that would indicate he was planning to do something about it.

When he'd written four or five lines, the sergeant turned and without explanation went into the kitchen. His wife appeared in the doorway, taking up her position as before. Matt heard the handle of a phone turn, a receiver being lifted, then the sergeant's voice asking for a Dublin number. A moment or two later, in a soft, patient voice, the sergeant said, 'You'll have to come inside now, Breda.' His wife backed in, closing the door behind her, making it impossible to hear the telephone conversation that followed.

At least it was to Dublin, Matt thought.

He picked up a leaflet about joining the Local Defence Force, recollecting in brief, uneasy snatches the exhausting drills and manoeuvres he'd done during the month he'd spent in the LDF training camp the summer before. He crumpled the leaflet, threw it into the smouldering grate, suddenly despairing of what he was sure would happen when he arrived: three or four gardaí leaping up and dashing out to the squad car; Josef in custody within the hour, on his way to the Curragh camp before the night was out.

The sergeant re-emerged, his chin extended upwards as he fastened his shirt stud.

'I take it you cycled here,' he said, his voice distorting as he extended his neck back to tighten his tie. 'Load up the bike. You may as well take the lift back.' He spoke in an offhand way, roughly strumming his lapels with his fingertips.

Driving along the empty road with the all-but-forgotten reek of petrol filling the car, Matt made a number of indirect attempts to find out what the sergeant intended to do. 'Depends,' he answered on almost every count, adding on each occasion that he would have to find out the lie of the land from Sergeant Cotton.

'Tell me, where are you from?' the sergeant asked after a long lull.

'Balbriggan. Balbriggan, County Dublin.'

'Is that part of the world any good for rabbits?'

Matt looked at him. 'I couldn't say, to tell you the truth.'

'Askeaton, where I'm from, is tops for rabbits.' He gripped the steering wheel tightly, leaned back, extending his arms the full of their length.

Outside the trees flitted by. The fields, wavy with summer growth, stretched across the flat, impassive landscape. Matt thought of his brothers, of being at home in Balbriggan, of shapeless days just slipping by.

'If it's alright with you I'll get out soon,' he said as soon as the Rathisland church spire came into view. Slowing down, the sergeant looked in the rear view mirror, turned to Matt and winked in a twitchy, conspiratorial way. 'It'd be better for all concerned if this was kept to ourselves.'

'That's what I was hoping. With being in the school and all.' He shrugged. 'Thanks for the lift back.' He smiled a little, relieved to find himself speaking to the sergeant in so unguarded a way, more relieved still when the sergeant said;

'We know where to get you if we need you, but I don't think we will.'

Matt stood, poised to bring his weight down on the pedal, all the while watching the car curving its way down onto the flat, burnished plain. A fresh, light breeze was steadily sweeping away what was left of the day's heat, clearing the way for the cool of the evening.

Chapter 14

Whenever Mrs Sheridan wasn't in at suppertime she left things in an advanced state of readiness. Salad, Matt figured when he saw a half-dozen or so scallion tips peeking out from beneath the battered tin-plate cover. Beside it, laid out like surgical instruments, was an array of tea accessories, cup, saucer, spoon, pot, cosy and caddy. Later, when she returned, there would be a spate of questions about whether he did, or didn't like this or that part of the supper. The trouble was that whatever he said would become law. Telling her he liked beetroot, as he'd done months back, had led to mounds of it appearing on his plate whenever there was salad for supper. Admitting that he didn't particularly care for radishes resulted in their never appearing again.

Still, just how fortunate he was to be in digs with Mrs Sheridan struck home every day, not only at suppertime but at lunchtime in school as well. There in Carmody's room, with the windows all steamed-up and condensation racing down the distempered walls, Carmody, Canning and Matt sat around Carmody's cluttered desk, packed lunches unfolded. Scarcely a day passed when Canning didn't monitor the pace at which Matt ate his lunch. Earlier in the year, Matt had offered him a sandwich after he'd remarked how tasty they looked. From then on, he delayed eating his own lunch, always the same dense, charcoal-coloured 'Emergency' bread with blackberry jam and, darting glances from behind the broadly spread pages of his *Irish Press*, would keep watch, hoping Matt might not finish the mound of homemade brown-bread ham sandwiches Mrs Sheridan had prepared.

Late for supper that evening, Matt lifted the tin cover, not at all surprised to find the plate awash with beetroot. Everything had a pinkish hue: the potato salad, the slices of hard-boiled egg, and the scallions. Ravenously hungry, he'd already begun eating when he spotted a neatly folded piece of paper propped against the milk jug. The word 'Abbeyleix' leapt out straight away. He was certain that it was in some way, he couldn't envisage how, connected with Josef, with what he'd done, with Madelene and Dixie. Hurriedly reading he was slow to accept that the note, in Mrs Sheridan's clear upright handwriting, was just a request to join in what she called 'a friendly' against the Abbeyleix tennis team the following day. 'Short notice,' it read, 'but with this glorious weather ...'

Nothing to be alarmed about, nothing at all. Matt told himself. But the initial sensation that there was had taken root, tightening his throat, making it almost impossible to swallow the food in his mouth.

The long bright evenings had seen the golf and tennis clubs swing into action again, though membership of the tennis club, despite Mrs Sheridan's recruitment drive, still didn't amount to more than a dozen or so people. The previous Saturday, one of the two tennis nets had been delivered to the house by Con O' Leary in a donkey and cart and under unrelenting instructions from Mrs Sheridan, dragged by him to the back garden where he eventually managed to drape it over the clothesline. She'd volunteered to repair it, following the arrival of a costly estimate to replace it from Elvery's Sports Equipment shop in Dublin. An accompanying letter, which she read to Matt shortly after it arrived, thanked her for her 'esteemed enquiry', going on to explain that 'the unusually high cost of the net was due to the difficulty of procuring such items under the present circumstances'. Mrs Sheridan was quick to meet the challenge. She took on the repair of the rotten net, cheerfully regarding the task as part of the war effort.

With his sights firmly set on going to Colls the following afternoon there was no question of joining in the 'friendly' against Abbeyleix. He lay on his bed after supper, the back of his head cupped in his hands, going through all the possible responses Madelene could have to Josef's arrest. Dixie will tell her I called, he thought, but that in itself is not going to … he shot up, everything suddenly stampeding ahead, soon all swarming around the notion that Dixie must have known where Madelene was and who she was with, that he'd … and Matt plonked back down onto his bed. 'Fuck,' he said aloud, 'dumb, fucken Dixie.' Not possible, he then thought, not possible, quick to reassure himself that Dixie didn't have the wit to stage something like that, confronted, in that same instant, by an image of him striding across the yard, not from the gizmo he was demonstrating to the two men, but from the sycamore, mouthing what he was about to ask Matt to do – mouthing, Matt now realized, what he'd been instructed by Rose and Statia to ask him to do.

It was about half past nine, a quietness about the world beyond his bedroom window that made it seem later.

Exhausted, he thought about taking off his shoes, about the marks they were making on the counterpane, unable, with the onset of sleep, to do anything about it. He remained aware in a dozy, distant way of the occasional sounds from outside, the resonating clack of footsteps below his window, voices from the far side of the Square, at the same time lured by sleep into a meandering tale in which the events of the day mingled in an obscure sort of way. At one point he thought the sergeant's wife was standing in the doorway of the bedroom, staring at him in the forlorn, long-faced way she had in the barracks. He raised his head briefly to confirm what he already knew was the absurd stuff of dreams, soon to drift back again into that mercurial world.

Around midnight he was woken by shouting, inter-mittent at first, rapidly growing louder and more frequent. He went to the window. The instant he saw the garda car in which he'd travelled from Abbeyleix parked outside the barracks across the Square, he drew the curtains, keeping a narrow chink open to see what was going on. The shouting had given way to argument, a tangle of words he strained to make out, able only to identify the odd phrase. 'Here, over here.' Words drowned out by other, louder words, 'Stay there'; 'This side.' As he adjusted to the darkness he saw Dixie standing beside the car in a heavy winter coat and Madelene getting out at the far side, the whole scene taking on distinct lines like a developing photograph.

Matt tiptoed back, then forward again, his whole body tensing when he saw Madelene, her hand clasped over her mouth, looking on as two gardaí, Sergeant Cotton and the Abbeyleix sergeant, forcibly tried to haul Josef out. Sergeant Cotton, rushed around and got in while the Abbeyleix ser-geant leaned into the car, soon to arch upwards, dragging Josef out by the hair and raising him to a standing position.

Hands flailing and head jerking wildly, Josef did his utmost to free himself. The Abbeyleix sergeant roared out suddenly, a high-pitched, feral cry, doubling up as his voice died out slowly in the otherwise eerily silent Square; Josef had kicked or kneed him in the groin. Sergeant Cotton tore around, tackled him at the waist and brought him to the ground. Matt could no longer see what was happening, but heard a boot thud against the car, then the same sound again, shortly followed by Josef's voice, hoarsely shouting something in German. Seconds later, still shouting, he was hiked up by both gardaí, flung against the car and held there, his arm twisted and his head pushed, face downwards, onto the bonnet. One of them produced a torch and shone it directly into his face. When Matt saw his rolling eyes, their whites bulging like those of a terrified horse, he recoiled into the darkness of his room.

When, after a moment or two of quiet, he returned to the window again he saw Josef being forced headlong into the pool of weak, ochre light coming from the opened door of the barracks, the hand of his twisted arm held fast between his shoulder blades. In that same light, Madelene, following timidly behind, appeared ill, fragile. Matt watched the play of her shadow in the light cast by the open door, exhaling slowly through his mouth when she, instead of following the others into the barracks, turned and left. Once out, she looked directly up at his window. He knew she could not see him, but nonetheless he stepped back. When, a minute or two later, he looked out again she was walking quickly past the garda car, unmistakably on her way over. Without giving it a second's thought he was on his way down, leaping whole sections of the stairs, diving for the door, bounding out onto the Square.

'No one came this morning. No one came to get him.

He's …' She pointed at the barracks, threw herself into Matt's arms the instant he reached her.

'God, you're shivering.' His grasp tightened.

'I kept looking up, hoping you'd see.' She pressed her head against his shoulder, her teeth chattering. 'It was …' She struggled for words, '… the worst was when …'

'Why did you have to come with him? I mean …'

'They said Dixie was to come to the barracks. Statia was hysterical. Rose too.' Words muffled by the closeness with which her face was pressed to his chest. 'It was all I could do, to come.' She began to sob. 'Josef threw things at them. And he boarded the loft trapdoor all up.'

Just then, Dixie, followed by the Abbeyleix sergeant, emerged from the barracks.

'Oh God.' Matt drew her even closer, images of Josef's crazed resistance flashing through his mind, cut through with an image of Costigan regaling him with cock-eyed talk of what lay in store for him if he was captured.

'Look, I know this might sound strange to say, Madelene, but Josef is much better off in there than he is with the likes of Costigan. I'm telling you. Honestly. They'll just bring him to the Curragh. And what's more, inform his family he's safe.'

Madelene said nothing, just nestled further in.

Over her shoulder Matt spotted the Abbeyleix sergeant heading towards them.

'Dixie's getting into the car.' He drew back from Madelene, nodded in the direction of the barracks.

'I'll drop you back now, whenever you're ready,' the sergeant said to Madelene from the distance, still coming towards them, slowing a little as he peered through the darkness at Matt, who, as Madelene edged away, whispered; 'I'll be out first thing in the morning.'

'Yes. No. A bit later. Rose and Statia will need settling. I'll be at the top of the lane at two.' She nuzzled into his chest. 'I can't think what I'd do if you weren't here.' She looked up at him, her whole face brimming with trust, the beginnings of a smile trickling across her lips.

Chapter 15

The thin, luminous beam of morning light shooting through the chink in the curtains through which Matt had watched Josef's arrest, extended right across the room, projecting a pool of wobbly light onto the opposite wall. From his bed, he followed the dancing dust particles it illuminated, all the while resisting thoughts that like a great, amassing army, were preparing to lay siege. Trying to hold out against them, he fixed on the unfamiliar sounds rising up the stairwell, the buckety racket of a tin, or a number of tins in the enamel sink, the cymbal-like clash of their lids, the noisy percussion of crockery and cutlery. At the same time, seeping through the gaps around the door was the rank, limey smell of water boiling, familiar in itself but now suffused with a peculiar, mildly chemical odour. Freshly shelled, hard-boiled eggs, he thought, or maybe one of those greenish-grey potions Mrs Sheridan concocted as an alternative to coffee. He foraged for his watch on the bedside table, surprised to discover that it was already half past nine.

Outside, the town was quiet, a stillness accentuated by the crisp clip clop of a passing pony and trap. It seemed as though everything was on hold, poised for the moment when word of Josef's arrest would break. He began to imagine that moment, people urgently stopping each other on the street, their faces agog with the news, standing on their neighbours' doorsteps, spilling the news.

Once downstairs he quickly identified the sounds and smells he'd been puzzling over. Mrs Sheridan, decked out in her white linen blouse, pleated tennis skirt and freshly whitened plimsolls was standing well back from the table sawing through a mound of sandwiches. Lined up to one side were three old biscuit tins. The smell of hard-boiled eggs, more concentrated now, mingled unevenly with her lavender talc, creating a chemist-shop atmosphere in which her whites gave her the look of a pharmacist.

Matt was sure she'd heard him leaving the house during the night, but wasn't at all surprised she didn't mention it. He'd observed, more or less from the day he'd first arrived, how intent she was on appearing discreet. But he'd since come to see that this didn't come easily to her. It required effort. It made her throw herself into what she was doing. It made her garrulous, anxious to fill every second, inclined to think aloud.

'With only one net, one court in action, the games will go on all day. Means lunch. No singles. Only doubles.' She spoke without looking up. 'They're here for eleven.' She leaned across the table and snapped up a tea cloth, unfolded it deftly, spread it over one of the open tins and pressed it down to form a lining.

Matt thought about the last time the Abbeyleix team came, about how apprehensive he'd been, about how decent a partner Wilkie Hodgins had turned out to be.

'Numbers aren't the problem I thought they were going to be,' she said crisply. It was, he figured, a delicate way of telling him she knew he mightn't want to give over a whole Saturday to playing tennis. 'Mrs O'Loughlin's son has a friend staying. They've agreed to play, and …'

'I can play as long as my game is over by lunchtime.' Matt cut in, his mind already made up, pleased to have a way of passing the morning, pleased too, in the already taut atmosphere created by his unexplained, late-night comings and goings, to strike a positive note.

'Oh good,' she smiled, 'means a second trip won't be necessary.' She pointed to the tins and the baskets, cheerily adding, 'Many hands make light work.'

There were at least a dozen people chatting in a loose, friendly way on the court without the net, when, laden down with tins and baskets Mrs Sheridan and Matt arrived. Mrs Sheridan swung into action straight away, directing him to go to what she called the pavilion with the food, while she and Rowena Harrington, began to organize people into teams.

Wilkie Hodgins wasn't there, a point Matt made to Nuala Gilmartin and Mary Lowry, who a few minutes previously had greeted him like a long lost friend. They looked at each other, each prompting the other to speak, before both spoke at once.

'He's not …'

'He's killed …'

'Just before Christmas.'

'Less than a month after he joined up. Poor Wilkie.'

Both nodded ominously. Matt was lost for words. He wanted to ask them where he'd been killed. He wanted to ask lots of things. How come he'd been sent straight into action? Did he have a family? He wanted to say how patient he'd been with him when they'd played the previous September. But he didn't feel entitled to ask these questions. It was as though the strictly enforced official prohibition on reporting deaths at the Front, or deaths in any way connected with the war, had somehow denied legitimacy to those deaths, making it unacceptable, even in an everyday, casual exchange to speak openly about them.

All three stood watching the doubles match in progress, a fast, concentrated game monitored by Rowena Harrington, who as a self-appointed umpire hollered rules and regulations from the sideline. The Rathisland team, Colum O'Loughlin and Paul Downey, both in their late teens, had underestimated the skill of the late-middle-aged couple picked to play them and were increasingly hard-pressed to keep pace.

On the way up to the grounds, Mrs Sheridan had mentioned this couple, Alf and Mil Stewart, several times, each time adding some new detail or other about them. Absorbed to the point of distraction by all that was going on in his own world, Matt was unable to muster much interest. But she persisted, explaining that they'd emigrated to Australia some thirty years previously and had recently returned to take possession of a large farm Mil had unexpectedly inherited from a distant relative.

Visibly irritated by the over-confident, quasi-sneering approach of the younger team Alf had obviously decided, though it wasn't at all in the spirit of things, to thrash them. He spent much of the time crouched in a semi squat, his jaw jutting forward, his eyes narrowed and manically fixed on them.

'Matt.'

Matt recognized Madelene's voice instantly. She stood, pressed against the perimeter fence directly behind him, one hand clasping the rusty chicken wire, the other extended through a gap, beckoning him over. He gestured to the gate, indicating with a circular movement of his finger, that he was on his way down. She shook her head – tight, emphatic movements, making it clear she wanted him to go directly over.

'The guards came back.' She paused to steady the tremor in her voice. 'Dixie's with them now.' She paused again. He'd never seen her so pale, so frightened. 'Matt. Josef is dead. I called to tell you, but …'

'Hold on. I'll be out in a sec.'

'Don't.' She glanced down the lane. 'We're going to Dixie, to the barracks. Later. I'll see you later.' She pointed at Rose and Statia, waiting a little distance away, their bikes, Madelene's in between, all facing in the opposite direction.

'How could he be dead?' Matt shook his head in disbelief.

But Madelene was already racing away. He dropped his racquet, tore out onto the lane, called after them to wait, unable to believe that they were pressing ahead, pretending not to hear. He went to follow them, stopped in his tracks by the realization that if he turned up at the barracks his part in Josef's arrest was sure to emerge.

The word *dead* slipped dryly through his lips. Nothing, he thought, nothing the gardaí had done the night before could have led to Josef's death. But maybe the struggle didn't end there, maybe his resistance got completely out of hand, maybe they … a possibility that was swept clean away by the crippling thought that if Madelene now found out he'd reported Josef she would hold him responsible for his death.

Some of the group glanced briefly in Matt's direction as he sidled in beside Nuala Gilmartin and Mary Lowry. All were engrossed in the match. He went to speak two, three times, eventually managing to say he'd just heard some shocking news.

'Oh?' Mary said, turning slightly in his direction, then instantly turning back to watch Alf shoot to the far side of the court to return a high, incoming lob.

'Yes. The pilot, the German pilot who the guards captured last night is dead.'

Mary looked to Nuala who was equally intent on the game.

'Yes, we heard that earlier.' She spoke without taking her eyes off the game.

'When we got here,' Mary chipped in.

'They …' Matt felt his arm move in a slow, semi-circular sweep of the group. 'They know he's dead too?'

Each waited for the other to speak.

'Yes. News travels fast.' Mary laughed in a clipped sort of way, closing her eyes briefly.

'Especially bad news,' Nuala added.

'Michael …' Mary nodded in the direction of the recently arrived bank clerk, '… heard about it getting the paper this morning. That's what Michael told us, wasn't it?'

'Yes, that's what he said …' Nuala's words trailed away, as if she wanted to wrap up the conversation, but Mary, for some reason, maybe because she didn't want to appear to be taking directions from Nuala, pressed on.

'He met Mrs Sheridan on her way home from the shops, where she'd heard it.'

Matt couldn't bring himself to believe that Mrs Sheridan knew about Josef's death before he'd even got up, knew about it all that time in the kitchen while he stood watching her packing the sandwiches and heating the flasks. And yet that, he realized, must have been the case. They all must know he'd reported Josef. What other reason could Mrs Sheridan have, could they all have, for not mentioning it to him?

He felt an overwhelming impulse to leave, to go somewhere, anywhere. He waited while Alf walked to the back of the court to serve, a moment that promised to command everyone's attention. Then, just as Alf spun the ball high into the air, he slipped away, heading straight to Colls to wait until Madelene returned.

The chestnut trees, lank and blizzard-blown throughout the winter, were now soft with new growth. The fields, rolling away into the distance, created a spaciousness that slowed down the pace at which thoughts, wild, desperate thoughts, were coursing through his head. Maybe, he thought, it would be better to tell Madelene everything, everything from the moment he arrived in the yard the previous afternoon. But Josef's death was there, an insurmountable obstacle, making just about anything he thought of saying to her seem limp and ineffectual.

He hadn't even reached the top of the lane leading down to Colls when he heard the familiar, mudguard rattle of her bike behind him.

'I knew you'd be here,' she shouted from the distance, leaning forward over the handlebars, her red cardigan in full sail, an eagerness about her that Matt could hardly bear to watch.

'Dixie's coming. It's alright. They'll be here ...' She flung the bike against the grassy bank, stepped over it, her hands rising as she approached. They tumbled into each other's arms; Madelene firmly closing ranks on the world, Matt abjectly adrift in that same world, certain it was only a question of time before she found out.

'Josef,' Madelene sighed, her whole body softening. 'They asked if we wanted to see him.'

'Who asked?'

'The sergeant. He's laid out in a cell at the back of the barracks.'

Matt hadn't thought about where he might be. He tried to envisage him laid out, but couldn't.

'What can have made him do such a thing?' Madelene drew her head back, looked up at Matt.

'Suicide?' Matt said tentatively, a possibility that had crossed his mind earlier but had been swept aside by the welter of other thoughts set in motion by the news.

She drew back further. 'What else? I mean yes. A tablet. Cyanide. The guards said it was something he'd brought with him, that all German pilots ...'

'Will we walk for a bit?'

They had only taken a few steps when Matt, afraid that all he was holding back was somehow going to burst out, turned to Madelene and in a matter-of-fact way said; 'I reported him. I told the gardaí where he was.'

Madelene said nothing. Nothing at all. She just glared at the ground. Matt put his arm around her waist, tried to draw her closer, startled by the force with which she resisted.

'I called out yesterday,' he said, glancing at her several times as he spoke, 'I called out yesterday after school. Dixie told me one of the cows had crossed the stream and got stranded. He asked me to go down and see.'

Madelene began to fall behind, her head even more bowed.

'But really it was Rose and Statia. They told him to ask me. I think they did anyway. And when I went I saw Josef wasn't gone. That he was there with you.'

'And that's what made you report him?' Madelene half-whispered, not so much asking Matt as telling herself.

'That. And knowing he'd be better off in ...' Matt's words trailed off. He went to put his arm around her waist again, freezing when in a low, panic-stricken voice, she said, 'Don't. Don't come near me.' She turned and began to walk back to where she'd left her bike, her pace quickening as she went. Matt watched for a moment or two then took off after her, circled around in front of her, grasped her forearms, tightening his grip when she struggled to break free.

'I won't be blamed for Josef's death,' he said forcibly, shaking her as he spoke. 'I won't have you blaming me for Josef's death.' He released her arms, flinging them carelessly away from him, altogether unprepared for the force with which her hand swung back and grabbed the centre of his face, one finger, nail first, piercing his eye. The pain shot through his head, fast as a bullet. And, immediately in its wake a violent throbbing sensation, an uncontrollable pounding that muffled what Madelene, now almost incoherent with tears, was saying about her aunts hating her mother, about how Matt had spied on her for them, about Josef, about her father, about someone called Ernie – people and things Matt had never even heard her mention before, all erupting in juddering gulps.

Matt pressed the palm of his hand over his injured eye, lifting it every few seconds, trying, but failing, to open it. Tilting his head to one side, he went about focusing his other eye, panicking when it too would not open. Prising the lids apart as he might a tightly clamped shell, he caught a drenched glimpse of Madelene picking up her bike, her red cardigan soon a quivering dot in the watery distance.

Chapter 16

Fifteen, twenty minutes later, with one hand still held over his injured eye, Matt pounded the knocker on Colls' door, pounded it again and again. He pressed his ear to the door, sure he heard movement inside, sure he heard Madelene coming. He began to rehearse what he was going to say. Heartfelt words, poised to open a trail back.

The tangling rose lurched out overhead, the petals of its tiny yellow flowers paling at the edges, those already fallen clustering around the boot scraper. He slumped down on the smooth, limestone step. Every sound, the swish of swallows as they swooped into the open gable window of the loft, the clank of a feeding pen in the lower yard, the split-second creak of an expanding window lintel, rekindled the hope that Madelene was about to appear. And then silence.

The faraway drone of a car came and went in waves, growing louder as it reached the top of the lane. All at once it was in the yard, Sergeant Cotton at the wheel, Dixie in the passenger seat. Matt stood up as they got out, expecting that

Dixie would come over to open the door and go in. He saw himself following Dixie down the hall to the kitchen, where he believed Madelene was, his heart sinking when Dixie waved from the distance, then hurried off in the direction of the farmyard. The sergeant, remaining at the car, rested his forearms on the roof and leaned forward.

'We took him from the milking.' He raised his chin, tilted his head towards Dixie. 'He was keen to get back.'

The sergeant began to drift over to Matt, passing his peaked cap from one hand to the other as he approached.

Matt didn't know what to expect. He knew the sergeant, but only to see. He had often cycled past himself and Madelene on the Castle Wall Road, his broad back bent over the narrow frame of his bike, his hand raised in an informal salute. But they'd never spoken. When he came to the school to try and find out who'd brought in the glove from the Messerschmitt, Carmody stuck close by his side, determined he wouldn't make any headway with his enquiries. Not that he put up much resistance. If anything, he seemed pleased to play along.

'The way it's after going is hard on everyone.' The sergeant came to a standstill a few paces away, his gaze wandering carelessly around the yard, then back to fix on Matt's injured eye.

Matt drew his lips tightly together and nodded.

'Course it's worst of all for the poor divil himself.' The sergeant lowered his head.

Fearful he was about to refer to his part in it all, Matt said nothing.

'You'd want to know ...' the sergeant paused as if to consider carefully what he was about to say, '... we'd want to tell you, at any rate, that it was known where he was all along. And, where he was being brought.'

Matt looked at him intently. The sergeant lowered his eyes, a shyness about him now. He threw his head to the side as if to underplay what he was saying.

'The lads above in Dublin had him followed from soon after he came. Once they caught wind of the crowd he'd fallen in with, they were thinking he'd lead to a few they'd been watching this long while.'

'Murt Costigan,' Matt blurted.

'Ah no, no, Murt wouldn't be up to those merchants.' He ran his splayed hand over his thinning hair, somewhat more at ease with himself now. 'Not at all, no. They landed him on Murt when they saw the net closing. A slippery customer by the name of Maguire. Tony Maguire. He'd have Murt in his pocket, if you know what I mean. Anyway, there's no taking Murt in now. He's well gone from these parts.'

'Gone?'

'The boat. He was tipped off last night. And no harm in that either. He's as well off, better off in England than locked up with the likes of what's above in tin town.'

'How could he have been tipped off?'

'They're some questions better left unasked.' He raised his eyebrows a little.

'I suppose,' Matt replied.

The sergeant placed his boot on the lowest step and leaned forward, drawing breath tersely before he spoke. 'I know only too well what's being said, but what I'm telling you is that we were waiting to move in on your man.' His lips clamped, giving his whole face an angularity, an expression that remained fixed.

'You were waiting to arrest Josef?' As Matt spoke, he felt the first trickle of what quickly became a torrent of relief.

'It was a matter of days, if that. We were waiting for the word from Dublin.'

'You were about to arrest him anyway?' Matt asked again.

'Like I'm telling you.' He pointed at Matt. 'You saying where he was yesterday only hurried it on by a day or two. We couldn't turn away from what a man of your standing reported.' The sergeant's expression softened to a smile.

As Matt's grasp on what the sergeant was disclosing tightened, a series of things began to click into place, the casual reception he'd got from the sergeant in Abbeyleix, the call he made to Dublin, the supposed sightings of the pilot the gardaí didn't seem to follow up. So much else, too. Matt glanced in the direction of the barn where Josef had stayed, slowly absorbing the notion that he'd been used as a decoy, an unsuspecting player in a strategy to identify members of the IRA intent on setting up links with the Abwehr.

'We'd have waited until he was on the way somewhere, like he was going to be.' The sergeant squared up. 'I would anyway. You know, waited until he was being brought somewhere else. Not to have those drawn into it that didn't need to be.' He glanced at the house.

'My advice to you, my advice to you now is to leave things be for the present.' He stole another look at the house. 'Let them to themselves awhile. You can take the lift back with me.' Holding his cap by the peak, he plonked it on his head and raised his other hand to press it into place at the back.

'No. No thanks. I have to stay. I have to make it clear, especially after what you've said.'

'That's between myself and yourself, a way of drawing it to an end.'

It took Matt a moment or two to take on board that the sergeant, in defiance of the procedure he was supposed to follow, was turning a blind eye to his involvement, his, and Dixie's, and seemingly Costigan's too.

'As I say you'd be best off leaving things as they are at

present.' The sergeant walked over to the car and waited, no change in his expression. Slowly, Matt began to follow him.

As they pulled out of the yard Matt's sights remained fixed on the house. Even if I stayed all night, he thought, Madelene still might not appear. He resolved to go to both Masses the following day, in which case he'd definitely meet her.

Out on the road, the wind whistled through the open front windows of the car, the same fume-filled Prefect in which Matt had travelled from Abbeyleix the previous evening and in which Josef had been brought to the barracks last night. He thought of the Abbeyleix sergeant's wife when he saw the yellowing holy pictures taped to the dashboard, the end one, an ascending saint, about to peel off. Soon he was busily piecing what the sergeant had told him into an explanation for Madelene, an explanation he raced through, rapidly arriving at the point where he'd say, 'So you see, I wasn't responsible for what happened. It was going to happen anyway.'

Just around the first corner, Rose and Statia, on their way out from the town, came into view, their heads craning forward with each downward pedal. The white basket on Statia's bike, tilting to one side with the weight of a rope bag full of groceries, was about to topple over any moment. They quickly got off their bikes and wheeled them up onto the embankment as the car approached, eager to acknowledge that they didn't trust themselves to remain in control as it passed. Matt waved, but they seemed unsure of who he was, their faces on high alert, framed to ask the other who it could be. Matt thought the sergeant might say something about them, maybe refer to their arrival at the station earlier in what he assumed was a bid to protest Dixie's innocence. But, acting as though he hadn't even seen them, he began to outline the arrangements for Josef's burial.

'In the graveyard above in Shrahanny. After first Mass in the morning,' he said in a firm, matter-of-fact way.

'But suicide? After committing suicide?' Matt turned towards him, about to point out that people who commit suicide can not be given a Catholic burial, when the sergeant cut in swiftly: 'What Father Finn said after the post-mortem above in the barracks this morning,' he leaned forward to wind his window up, 'is that no one can tell for sure that he did it, that he could have repented at the last minute.'

'Of course. No. It's the right thing to give him the benefit of the doubt.' Words Matt rushed at the sergeant, regretting he'd questioned the arrangement in the first place.

'Aye, and about him being the right persuasion too.' The sergeant gripped the steering wheel with both hands, extending them until he was driving the car like a figure in a child's drawing. 'The pity of it was that he didn't listen to what we were telling him last night. When we came for him. We said it a thousand times if we said it once. Kept saying it to him. There's nothing going to happen to you. Nothing. But he wouldn't open the trapdoor. Just kept piling stuff up against it. Old tackle. Harnesses, anything he could lay his hands on. You see, you wouldn't know what the likes of Maguire had told him would happen if he was brought in. Anyway,' he nodded firmly, intent, it appeared, on drawing it all to a close.

Large charcoal clouds were swelling overhead, their spangled edges thinning to wisps of silvery light. By the time they reached the Square, the first, heavy droplets of the fast-approaching downpour were already falling.

'Take my advice and look after that eye.'

'Thanks for the spin back,' Matt shrugged, 'and for everything.'

He rushed into the house, stopping dead, when, in the

hall mirror, he unexpectedly glimpsed his eye. He moved closer. His eyelid was swollen beyond recognition. Nothing of the white remained. He wondered if he should cover it or if that would draw more attention to it, concerns that catapulted his thoughts forward to the following morning when he would meet Madelene at Mass. He headed for the Fly-tight, sidetracked by the thought of the muslin-covered haunch of ham Mrs Sheridan put into it after she'd made the sandwiches.

He whiled away the rest of the afternoon, looking out his bedroom window watching the murky, brown water rush down the crisscrossing gullies on the Square. Around suppertime he saw Mrs Sheridan with some of the Abbey-leix team, Mary Lowry, Nuala Gilmartin, Alf and Mil Stewart all still in their whites, wheeling their bicycles across the Square, wholly abandoned to the torrents unrelent-ingly belting down on them. Soon he could hear them in the hall below, Mrs Sheridan directing them upstairs, telling them there would be a cup of hot tea ready as soon as they'd changed. 'Or something stronger for those with a taste for it,' she added perkily. To which Alf chuckled, 'Count me in for that.' Two, three, four snippets of conversation reached Matt from the clattery warmth of the kitchen, crisscrossing voices laced with skittish laughter as Mary Lowry and Nuala Gilmartin playfully fought for a space on the Aga bar. There was no talk of Josef, of death or indeed of war. The rain pro-vided all the adversity necessary to keep spirits up.

Chapter 17

Arriving in plenty of time for first Mass, Matt chose a pew towards the rear, a position from which he would be able to observe everyone entering the church. A mild scent of lilac, suffused with burning candle wax, filled the dark, vaulted interior. The organist, Carmody's sister-in-law, whose playing Mrs Sheridan often criticized, was practising scales.

In the corner of his eye, as he genuflected, Matt caught a glimpse of Josef's coffin, not in the usual place at the top of the centre aisle, but in front of the side altar to the left. Unwilling to believe what he thought was a swastika flag draping the coffin, he sidled out of his pew and slipped into one further up. There it was, a swastika as real as the one on the Messerschmitt, its flame-red background accentuated by the glow of the perpetual adoration lamp.

The organ scales, light and unvarying for the most part, began to ramble down to the bass clefs, breaking into the opening bars of the entry hymn, a practice run the organist repeated several times. Matt tried to work out where the swastika flag could have come from. He raised his head as far as possible, craned this way and that in an effort to see if it had been made up for the occasion. He wanted to move closer, get a better look at it, but the church was beginning to fill up and besides, he wanted to remain in a position from where he could spot Madelene.

The organist heralded the opening hymn, 'Soul of My Saviour', delicately sounding the first few notes in single keys, then pounding it out in anticipation of rousing the congregation into song. Rose and Statia ambled up the centre aisle in their usual way, Statia gazing about, intrigued, as though she'd never been in a church before.

'Today's Mass,' Father Finn solemnly announced, 'will be celebrated for the repose of the soul of the young man whose remains have been brought here this morning.' Statia and Rose, still manoeuvring themselves into a pew, looked back down the aisle several times, confirming Matt's belief that Madelene, attuned to the speculation about Josef's capture and death smouldering all around, decided to slip into a pew at the very back. Two marbelized pillars made it impossible to see everyone in those last few pews, but he felt sure she was there.

When Father Finn stepped up onto the pulpit to deliver his sermon, Matt was expecting him to say something about Josef, figuring he'd probably begin by pointing to the suffering inflicted by war. Instead he launched into a dramatic homily on mercy and forgiveness, quoting Portia from *The Merchant of Venice*, 'The quality of mercy is not strained …', leading Matt to wonder if he might be speaking directly to him and Madelene, taking solace in the impact so passionate a sermon about forgiveness might have on her.

Father Finn did not mention Josef by name, or even by reference, beyond announcing at the outset that the Mass was being offered for the repose of his soul. With Josef's poisoned remains no more than a few feet away from the pulpit, this struck Matt as peculiar. But as the Mass went on it occurred to him that he was probably prohibited from mentioning anything that might refer the congregation to what was going on in the world at large.

When Mass ended, the undertaker, Paudie Barton, together with his thickset, red-haired sons, hoisted the coffin up, tucking the overhanging sections of the flag in underneath before easing it down onto their shoulders. A burial after the earlier, less popular, of the two Masses was unusual. Still, hordes of people had turned out, now all standing about in the drizzly churchyard, the story of Josef's death hissing around like a burning fuse wire. Talk of Matt's involvement was apparent everywhere, in the awkwardly stolen glances in his direction, in the undisguised gaping of shrunken, mountainy men, in the brief, searching smiles of their womenfolk. Too caught up in his search for Madelene, he paid little or no attention. He saw Rose and Statia standing on the side-entrance step. As he made his way over, they edged forward a little, Statia to the fore, smiling with a sort of feathery lightness, her eyelids lightly drawn over her eyes.

'Mr Duggan,' Rose, partly shielded by Statia, said, her head angled, her freckled hand outstretched as though to sympathize with him.

'So awful …'

'Awful.' Statia placed her splayed hand on her breast-bone, turned to Rose, 'so hard to understand.'

'And just when Madelene had to go.'

There was a sudden hush as Father Finn, sprinkling the coffin with Holy Water, began the funereal prayers. Rose and Statia lowered their eyes simultaneously.

'What do you mean?' Matt said, prompting Statia to lean forward, place the tips of her fingers on his forearm and whisper, 'I'm sure she …' What followed was for the most part drowned out, as the congregation joined Father Finn in prayer. Matt heard the words 'unexpected leave' and then 'Larry', Madelene's father's name, and 'all so last-minute'. Heard enough to know Madelene had left. Rose and Statia responded loudly to every invocation of the litany into which Father Finn had launched.

Hopping from one foot to the other, Matt waited for an opportunity to question them, eventually managing to squeeze the word 'when' into a gap in the prayers. Statia and Rose looked at each other, creating the impression that they didn't understand what they were being asked. 'When did Madelene leave?' Matt demanded impatiently. They continued to look at each other, their faces filling with alarm as though Matt had just broken news of Madelene's departure to them.

'For how long? When is she coming back?'

'As soon as she gets the chance, I'm sure.' Statia smiled blithely, reached out, rested her fingers on Matt's forearm. He snapped his arm away and strode over to join in the cortège, now edging out of the churchyard.

Shuffling along behind the hearse, he heard, but didn't respond to, comments about the sadness of Josef's death, about the size of crowd that had turned up for the funeral, about the change in the weather.

The swastika flag was removed and folded by Paudie Barton at the graveside then handed ceremonially to the eldest of his sons. Father Finn sprinkled the coffin with Holy Water as it was lowered into the grave, the rhythmic liturgy, '*Pater et Filius, et Spiritus Sanctus …*' trailing to a close as it hit the ground. Matt stood a few yards back, part of a loose-knit group of men that were talking among themselves about cattle prices. He was calm, calm in a resigned, numb way.

Alone on the Castle Wall Road after supper with fragments of the many letters he'd begun to Madelene that afternoon coursing pell-mell through his head, he despaired of ever being able to put his case convincingly to her. He had reported Josef. Josef had committed suicide. Everything else, no matter what way it was put, was secondary. He thought about what she'd said about her aunts hating her mother, about him spying on her for them, about Josef, about her father, about someone called Ernie.

Late into the evening, with the light fading, he turned to go back. Coming to the top of Colls' lane after about a half an hour or so, he dawdled for a bit, imagining in a way he knew was fanciful, that something might happen. Anything, anything at all that might release him from the dead hand of futility choking his every thought. But nothing did. The lane, dark and unyielding in the dusk, only deepened the hopelessness he felt. He walked on, still trying to piece a letter to Madelene together, still failing at every turn.

Less than a half-mile from the town he heard a pony and trap approaching from behind, the crack of the drivers whip clear and sharp in the night air. Afraid he might not be seen, he stopped and positioned himself close to the verge, then watched it approach, the roll of its wheels growing louder, its lamp lights glinting on the tackle brasses. As it drew closer he saw that it was Colls' pony. Someone, he thought, must have borrowed it, sure that Dixie would not drive the pony that hard, using the whip every few seconds. But it was Dixie, Dixie with Madelene seated at the other side, staring into the darkness ahead, a Travelight on her lap. And behind, Rose and Statia each with her hand on her hat, holding it down. Matt stepped out, just as they'd passed, roared, 'Stop.' He started running after them, roared 'Stop' again. He stood in the middle of the road waiting for them to slow down, unable to bring himself to accept that they were belting ahead, the crack of the whip and the roll of the wheels already growing feint in the distance. For a second or two he wondered if he'd seen them at all, a notion that quickly gave way to the realization that they were on their way to the night train. Rose and Statia had lied to him when they'd told him Madelene had gone. It was a ploy to keep him away. He sat down on the grassy verge, defeated to the point of stupefaction.

Chapter 18

Carmody wasn't at the funeral Mass or the burial, so Matt didn't get an opportunity to take stock of his response to what had happened. Not that he was, by that stage, particularly concerned about what Carmody did or did not think. There was less than a fortnight to go to the summer holidays. Nothing mattered now, except getting out of Rathisland.

When, on Monday morning, Matt went in to collect the roll book, it was business as usual, with Carmody drawing on his ash-laden cigarette as he crossed the room to the rickety roll-book cupboard.

'I hear the minors took a terrible hammering yesterday.'

'Did they?' Matt replied, adding, as he took the roll book, that the rain will have gone against them.

'True for you, but it wasn't the weather they lost to,' Carmody quipped as Matt left, arching his thick eyebrows until they met the shock of wiry hair extending out over his forehead, attempting, as he often did, to ply his parting words with a significance they didn't have. Six, seven, eight months previously, Matt might have puzzled over such a remark, but now saw it as just another of Carmody's ploys to divert attention away from all that he wished to conceal about himself and his place in the scheme of things.

The day dragged interminably. Pádraig Costigan, sullen from the outset, scowled at anyone who showed enthusiasm in answering any of the questions Matt put to the class. It wasn't confrontational enough to act on, just a low-intensity war he would maintain for most of the two remaining weeks. It struck Matt as ironic that the Costigan boys' position was, as a result of their father's departure for England, now similar to that of several others in the class, boys whose fathers they'd been quick to denounce as traitors because they'd taken up jobs in wartime production plants in the UK. Matt knew they were just parroting what they'd heard at home, but that didn't lessen the impact of their accusations. Afraid of being identified as the sons of 'traitors', none of those whose fathers had taken up these jobs ever responded.

Later in the week Pádraig left a note on Matt's desk, just dropped it right in front of him and trooped off in his noisy hobnailed boots. Written on an unevenly torn piece of copybook paper, and signed 'Mrs Marie Costigan', it announced that she was coming in to see him after school the following day. Matt had seen her with her husband Murt from time to time, but had never spoken to her.

Canning laughed when Matt told him she was coming in. He claimed she had charged onto the pitch during a hurling match some years previously and broken one of the referee's front teeth with an umbrella handle. Matt prepared himself for the worst, imagining she was going to hold him accountable for her husband's fate.

'The best thing,' Canning advised, 'is to let her do all the talking. You just listen and say as little as possible.'

It wasn't so much the prospect of an attack that bothered Matt. It was the revisiting of events from which, minute by minute, hour by hour, he was desperately trying to crawl away. He hadn't been able to bring himself to explain to anyone, Canning included, what had happened. And that despite the many friendly, if awkwardly contrived, opportunities Canning gave him.

'I won't hold you a minute,' Mrs Costigan said, turning to shut the door of the classroom, warning her children whom she'd left outside that she'd beat them black and blue if there was as much as one word out of any of them. Remaining close to the door, she spoke in a raised voice, releasing what she had to say as though she'd been rehearsing for some time.

'The way it is, there's no money coming into the house until Thursday week at the earliest. He'll be wiring some then.' She looked at Matt defiantly, accusing him, or so it seemed, of pretending not to know what she was getting at. 'That's over a week away.'

'If you want to borrow some, I mean I can ...' He spread his hands, indicating his willingness to lend her some, relieved to be getting away so lightly. She swung her head to one side, even more defiant as she said, 'Yes, three pound.'

'I don't have that much with me, but I can send it home with one of the boys tomorrow after school.'

'You can make it five.' She pursed her lips firmly as if to impress on Matt she wouldn't be prepared to negotiate.

He hesitated. Five pounds was a week's wages, and still it seemed a small price to pay to be rid, not so much of her, as the torment her visit rekindled.

'You'll have it tomorrow,' he said, walking towards her in an attempt to usher her out.

'It'll be paid back,' she said, now out in the hall grabbing the wrists of two sticky-faced children while edging a third forward with her knee.

'That doesn't matter,' Matt said, partly because he knew the money wouldn't be returned, partly because her plight seemed so wretched, but mostly because he felt guilty.

The following afternoon, looking out the classroom window after school, the same one from which he'd mistakenly thought he'd seen Madelene waiting outside all those months ago, he watched Pádraig open the envelope he'd just given him. A crowd gathered around as he held the five-pound note up, a triumphant air about him. Matt looked on calmly, thoughts about how it would be reported to every home in the town that afternoon, how it would be interpreted, all just flowing through his head, hardly causing a single ripple. He was beyond caring and would remain so for the rest of his time in Rathisland.

Canning, who'd begun to suspect that Matt might not be returning in September, went out of his way to put a smiley spin on things. He assured him he'd have no bother with the probationary business, which Matt knew to be the case, if only because Carmody wouldn't want to be seen to know anything about what had happened.

'That's something, at any rate,' Matt replied, which was as near as he ever got to saying anything to Canning about it all.

Matt's plan to deliver his letter of resignation to Father Finn by hand, rather than post it, was foiled by the recent return of the parish priest whom Father Finn had been replacing. Father Finn was still serving in the parish, but was now no longer the school manager. And this, Matt felt, was for the best, because whenever he thought about explaining his decision to Father Finn, he was confronted by the image of Madelene, her aunts and Dixie, emerging through the gloaming, their faces straining forward, their eyes, glassy and unblinking, a scene in which he himself remained paralyzed.

Mrs Sheridan, well aware of the turn things had taken in Matt's world, was her usual discreet self, though the suppers she left before going to this or that meeting, the golf club, the tennis club and so forth, were spectacularly large, much larger than the already large suppers she'd served all that winter and spring. Thick, clove-studded slices of ham, hard-boiled eggs, scallions, lettuce and beetroot to beat the band, servings so large that the tin-plate cover sat on top like an ill-fitting hat. During those final days, Matt came to see those suppers as a language of sorts, a form of coded support and sympathy for which he was very grateful. When he told her he wouldn't be returning in September, which he didn't do until a few days before he left, she was reassuringly unsurprised.

'It's good to get experience elsewhere, good to move about, see other … Benny and I lived in so many places and I can't say I regret one moment. No, not one.'

'Thanks,' he said, though nothing she'd actually said called for thanks.

There was already a slight seasonal turn on the early July day Matt left Rathisland. The change was only barely perceptible, a stillness in the late afternoon which seemed to rise from the very landscape itself, a slowing of growth, the first burst of spring and early summer already spent. He had his Gladstone packed and ready early on, planning to walk to the station to catch the evening train. Mrs Sheridan, though she wasn't there herself, had, unknown to him, arranged for Con O'Leary to collect him and bring him to the station. 'That way,' she explained in the note she left, 'there will be time for a bite to eat before leaving for the train.' The note was propped up by a plate piled so high that it hadn't been possible to place the tin cover on top.

Chapter 19

Willow Road, Clonskeagh, Dublin. Throughout their childhood, Matt's daughters, Carrie and Emer never tired of asking their mother, Effie, to tell them about how she and Matt met. And Effie never tired of telling them. She would spin the story out, moment by moment, her voice full of mystified wonder, her eyes widening in anticipation of revealing this or that detail. It didn't bother her that what she was telling them was inaccurate. If Matt was there he might point this out in a playful sort of way, and, if given the opportunity, would go on to explain that the account Effie was giving was roughly, very roughly, based on their second rather than their first meeting. Confident that they would opt for her version, not least because of the captivating way in which she was telling it, Effie would say in a vague, slightly wry way; 'I don't remember actually meeting you. You were there in the background, I remember that, but we didn't meet, not in the way we met later.'

'So we met for the first time on the street,' Matt might

say, 'we met on the street and you had no difficulty entering into a conversation with a complete stranger, no difficulty in agreeing to go to a café with him a minute later?'

'You weren't a complete stranger,' Effie would say, emphasizing the word *complete* while smiling reassuringly at Carrie and Emer.

'That's the point I'm making. If I wasn't a complete stranger then it wasn't the first time we met.'

And Effie would smile, affectionately accepting his reluctance to look beyond the facts.

Emer and Carrie enjoyed this set-piece exchange so much that when it ended and Effie had resumed describing what she regarded as their first meeting, they'd often try to revive the controversy.

'You weren't a *complete* stranger,' they'd say, imitating Effie's intonation.

It was, as Matt accurately recalled it, April 1945. He was walking down Nassau Street on his way to College Green to catch a tram.

It was, Effie would usually begin, a warm spring day. I remember looking up and seeing fresh green leaves on a branch overhanging the Trinity railings.

It was a Saturday, about four o' clock. Matt had, as he recalled it, spent the afternoon in town and was on his way home.

In the distance I saw a man walking in my direction, a very handsome man wearing an unimaginably smart raincoat with a paisley scarf. The height of fashion.

Matt recognized the girl walking towards him.

Hello, he said as he approached, but I didn't recognize him so I quickened my step.

'It's Evelyn, isn't it?' he said, a bit put out that she didn't seem to know who he was.

I could hardly believe that he knew my name. I can't think what must have gone through my head. I then realized I knew him from somewhere but couldn't immediately remember where. I wondered if my lipstick was smudgy, if I'd put some on in the café.

'It's Matt. Matt Dugan,' he said, a little uncomfortable at having to introduce himself.

As soon as he said his name I remembered who he was, though I'd never actually spoken to him beyond saying good morning or good afternoon.

'Remember?' Matt smiled.

Yes of course, I said, you stayed with my mother, the year before last, when you taught in the school.

Matt was absolutely certain he asked her at that point how her mother, Mrs Sheridan, was, absolutely certain too, that, eyes-downcast, she told him in a low, but nonetheless matter-of-fact voice, her mother had died over a year previously. But this never ever featured in the account of the meeting she gave to Carrie and Emer.

His immediate response on learning that Mrs Sheridan had died, he clearly recalled, was disbelief. He foraged awkwardly for words. 'I'm sorry, very, very sorry to hear that,' he eventually said, and feeling the inadequacy of those words, asked Evelyn if she was free to go somewhere for a cup of tea.

He asked if I'd like to have tea with him, suggested we go to the Monument Creamery, where, as it happened, I'd just been having tea with Dilly Fagan and Maureen Malone. They were still there when we arrived. You can't imagine their expressions. There I was scarcely gone five minutes arriving back with the handsomest man in Dublin …

They didn't feature in Matt's version, but if prompted, he would, in an offhand way, admit to having noticed them, in particular the way one of them was fidgeting with the long necklace she was wearing, glancing in Effie's and his direction every few seconds while pretending to be absorbed in conversation with the other one. What he remembered best was the composure, the self-possession with which Effie spoke about her mother's death, describing in a calm, even-handed way her many dealings with the doctors, her face brightening as she related how they were sure Mrs Sheridan would make a full recovery from what he gathered had been a fairly minor stroke. 'She'd lost the will to live,' Effie said quietly, explaining how close her parents had been, smiling a little as she described the gusto with which her mother threw herself into things after her father died. Matt thought of the tennis net draped over the clothesline, unaware that he was being calmly guided back to Rathisland, allowed to look at everything that happened from a safe distance, something he'd been unable to do for more than a few moments at a time since he left two years previously.

And although he didn't propose until well over a year later, I knew in my heart that this was the man I was going to marry. It's something you know, regardless. At this point Carrie and Emer were inclined to drift off as though searching for that part of themselves which would 'know, regardless'.

He asked if we could meet again, some evening the following week, Wednesday maybe, he said. I agreed, but then remembered, or pretended to remember, that I had another engagement. Carrie and Emer enjoyed this pretending to remember bit immensely. *Saturday, are you free on Saturday to go to a film, maybe? he said. After a moment's thought I said yes.*

If at this point in the story Effie left out 'after a moment's thought', they'd stop her in her tracks, forcefully reminding her of the omission as though she'd broken an important rule in a board game. Sometimes, she might pause before saying it as if unable to remember what came next, paving the way for Carrie and Emer to rush in, their faces brimming with the words before they blurted them out ... 'After a moment's thought, you said yes.'

Cinemas, you have to remember, weren't just cinemas in those days. There was a restaurant and, in the bigger ones, like the Savoy there was often a dance band with a space for dancing in front. A whole evening's entertainment. Saturday came. I was exactly on time so I stayed on the tram for a further two stops then slowly made my way back to the Savoy, almost twenty minutes late.

Matt recalled looking down O'Connell Street, down towards the bridge, sure, as the minutes went by and there was no sign of her, that she wasn't going to turn up. He did not expect her to come from the other direction. Then there she was, more alive than anyone else on the street, or indeed in the whole city. A moment or two later, as she waited in the middle of the foyer while he queued for tickets, he saw her image reflected in the glass of the ticket booth. She had taken a small round powder case out of her handbag and was checking her appearance in the mirror. The mirror was no larger than the base of a glass so she had to move her head in several different directions to check on everything, her hair, her earrings, her lipstick.

Less than twenty minutes in the cinema, we turned to each other at the exact same instant, both of us realizing, without exchanging a single word, that we'd prefer to be outside in the café listening to the music, dancing, talking, getting to know one another. And that's exactly what we did. We just stood up and left. And as quick as you can say Jack Robinson we were at a table a few feet from the band with the musicians smiling in our direction, playing away as though just for us.

There was no doubt in Matt's mind about what happened when they went into the cinema. The familiar rooster call, followed by the brassy boom of the Pathé News signature tune led straight into a snappy piece about an English family who had lived in the Australian outback for years without making any contact with the world beyond. What followed this was so unexpected, so unlike anything he'd ever seen that at first he couldn't make sense of it. A long line of unbelievably emaciated people, their eyes dead and faces strangely expressionless, were being led past what appeared to be a long, low hut. Slowly it began to emerge that the scene was connected with the war, that it was in fact part of the war, that those shaven, skeletal creatures had been found in what the self-assured, fast-talking presenter called a 'concentration camp', a place of mass execution constructed and administered by the Third Reich. The scene shifted to a dark, treeless landscape in which a number of figures standing at the edge of a cliff or a quarry seemed to be pitching human remains over the edge. Another change of scene revealed a mound of splayed bodies, onto which other bodies were landing every few seconds. Matt felt a sudden tightening sensation around his temples. His stomach began to heave. He turned to Effie, about to announce that he needed to go out and get some air, when she stood up of her own accord and pointing to the end of the row hurriedly indicated that she was on her way out. Several others stood up to leave too. He clearly recalled that once outside they didn't seem able to speak about what they'd seen beyond saying how terrible, how sickening it was. He remembered the sensation of having witnessed something that lay beyond the scope of language, of having journeyed to a part of the human psyche which had momentarily altered his entire view of humanity. And with that came a low-lying, inexplicable sense of guilt.

He couldn't say about what, about not knowing maybe, about having a comic book idea of the war, about the safety and security of his own life.

When the waiter came we ordered tea, the full tea, sandwiches, scones, cakes. There were some couples dancing, American service men, all spruced up, smart as a shiny sixpence. And there was a feeling that the war would be over any minute. The band were all dressed up too. They were in tuxedoes and everyone was enjoying themselves. Then they began to play this song. I'll never forget that moment. We'd only just started to tuck into our tea, but we left it and stood up to dance. Even now I feel a little dizzy when I recall the way we spun around the dance floor, just us with the rest of the world all blurred and out of focus.

As Matt recalled it, the waiters in the tearoom were very busy. Quite a while passed before they managed to place an order for tea and it was so long coming that they decided to dance.

And here, or hereabouts, their stories would finally begin to merge.

Matt could dance quite well, but Effie was a magnificent dancer, so she danced for both of them, effortlessly guiding them around the dance floor, her frock fanning out on the wide swerving turns, her head tilting back flamenco-style, her every movement perfectly timed to catch the shifting, often unpredictable sound of the slinky Spanish brass. Matt could have told her the name of the song, but, as she would reveal a few moments later, it didn't occur to her to ask him. Instead, when the dance ended, she went directly over and asked the permanently smiling piano player.

'It's called "South of the Border", ' she announced as she sat down, her face brimming with excitement, the plan to buy the sheet music already in place.

'I know, and I really like it, but I'd never have guessed that you'd like it. I mean it's different, a bit below the kind of music … you know, the stuff you've being doing in the conservatoire.'

Effie's face filled with alarm, but only for a split second, giving way dramatically to exasperation. 'My poor mother, it's heartbreaking the way she told everyone I was in the conservatoire in Basle. Matt, I was a down-the-line govern-ess. I took piano lessons once a week in the small academy in the nearby town, almost forty miles from Basle. That's it. That's the sum of it.' And she looked at him defiantly as if to say *you can take it or leave it, it's up to you*. Matt was bowled over by the command she had of her own situation. It struck him that she was clearing the decks, ensuring that if they continued to meet, which already seemed likely, the past would not harbour any ghosts.

Reflecting on that afternoon, as Matt occasionally did down the years, he could see that Effie was determined to move beyond her mother's death. Beyond that well-disguised sense she had of being profoundly alone in the world, the legacy of parents who had both been effectively cut off from their own families. They had, it transpired, been denied a Roman Catholic wedding until her father, whose family were Church of Ireland, agreed to undertake a course in Catholic doctrine that would equip him to bring up whatever chil-dren they might have as Catholics. He held out against this diktat for years, eventually succumbing when he and Mrs Sheridan were in their early forties. Effie liked to believe that this did not lead to a cooling of relations between her mother and her original family, yet she could count on one hand the number of times she'd met her cousins. Equally, Mrs Sheridan's relations with her husband's family had been irrevocably damaged by the whole thing.

'When my mother moved back to Rathisland that priest was very good to her, Father … you know, the one who did the *Hamlet*.'

'Finn.'

'Yes. Father Finn. And he found her a lodger.' She smiled broadly and pointed at Matt.

'Which is why you had a tantrum when you came home at Christmas?'

'You were in my room. My mother had put you in my room and never told me.'

Matt laughed, all the while acclimatizing to the shifts taking place in his own immediate past, his view of Mrs Sheridan, of Father Finn, of himself. And there was an extraordinary freedom in this, not so much the freedom of being able to think about that past without wincing, but the freedom of realizing that the past itself was negotiable, that it was not a life sentence. Effie had set the pace for the forward march and he was only too pleased to join in, soon to begin unburdening himself of all that had happened in Rathisland. He told her about Madelene, about Josef's death, and the web of misunderstandings surrounding it.

Not a word of this featured in the version of the afternoon Effie presented to Emer and Carrie.

I still remember the three-tiered plate stand, she would say dreamily. On the top a cream puff, a slice each of Battenberg and marble cake, a piece of fruitcake and an éclair. On the next plate down, five of the freshest scones you ever saw. And beneath on the bottom plate, thin, white-bread ham sandwiches, crusts cut off, and I can't tell you what a treat smooth, white bread was at the time. We chatted about this and that, all the time listening to the music, ready to leap up and take to the floor whenever we heard something we liked. I kept on hoping they'd play 'South of the Border' again and was thrilled beyond belief when a few moments after I'd come back from the powder room, the band leader, Mr Mauricini himself, announced that there had been a request for Miss Evelyn Sheridan. Of course I knew full well who had made the request. But all the same I looked around the room not owning up to knowing straight away, keeping the element of surprise for the moment he would tell me, which he did just as we got up to dance. Everyone stood back as we made our way out. The dance floor was all ours. So was the song.

At this point in the story Effie would often stand up and go over to the piano and in a slow, light, deliberate sort of way begin to pick out the notes, all the time smiling as though she was fully conscious of the wildly romantic spin she was putting on that story. Not that the evening was without romance, not at all, but the greater part of it, had, as far as Matt was concerned, taken place on terra firma.

Effie did not so much want to remember it differently as to relate it differently to Carrie and Emer, a point she would readily acknowledge if Matt brought it up as he sometimes did, in a teasing sort of way, when Emer and Carrie were not around.

'I know, I know,' Effie might say, 'but they need to go into life believing and hoping and that won't happen if they're weighed down with stories of dead pilots and concentration camps.'

There was no option but to agree.

Chapter 20

Dawdling over the death column in the newspaper, as had been his habit for the best part of thirty years, Matt was absent-mindedly piecing together the story each announcement told, when he happened upon a story he already knew.

Coll (Rathisland, Co. Laois) December 12, 1970 (peacefully), Richard (Dixie), after a short illness bravely borne, sadly missed by his sisters Rose and Anastatia, niece Madelene, grand nephew Maurice, friends and relatives. Rest in peace. Funeral today (Saturday) after 11 o'c Mass in St Loman's church. Burial immediately afterwards in Shrahanny cemetery.

Matt leaned back on his chair, reread it, his mind already made up to go to the funeral, even though he could not, at that late stage, hope to make it in time to attend the Mass. And so it was, an hour and a half later, he pulled up and parked outside the house he'd stayed in almost thirty years ago, ready to join in the cortège when it arrived. Swept back over those years by a torrent of memories, he did not notice the approach of the funeral until it was a few yards behind him. Leaning forward towards the wing mirror, he watched the slow approach of the hearse, anticipating that Madelene, Rose and Statia would be in the car following directly behind. He controlled the urge to turn and look, disappointed to discover as it passed, that it was a funeral limousine with darkened, opaque glass. He looked for an opportunity to join in the long procession of cars that followed, but the hearse was moving so slowly that there was no gap. Eventually, he joined in at the tail end and edged along behind at a snail's pace.

The lower stretch of the road leading up to Shrahanny cemetery had been widened in places. Not much, just enough to allow two cars travelling in opposite directions to pass without slowing to a virtual standstill. Nearer the cemetery it reverted to the boreen it always was, its raised centre ridge mossy, its two deep furrows intermittently waterlogged. All the parking spaces around the entrance to the cemetery were taken so he had to drive well beyond it.

The most routine transactions – turning off the engine, heaving himself out of the car, closing the door – felt significant, each a preliminary move in an invasion of the past. The now empty hearse, backed up to the open gate of the small hillside cemetery, was old, but so highly-polished that its surfaces mirrored the shifting December skyscape, whisking it up to appear like marauding storm clouds. Reflected darkly in those surfaces, Matt's approach appeared laboured, his open coat flapping like the wings of a large bird.

In the distance, forty-five, maybe fifty people, mostly men, trailed in a dark broken line behind the coffin. The bearers, hands clamped tightly on each other's shoulders, were listing to the right, now and then shuffling to a standstill as they manoeuvred their way along the narrow path.

Directly behind, all muffled up and huddled together were three figures, and although he couldn't see their faces, Matt knew that the more upright one in the centre was Madelene. Linked on either side were Statia and Rose, both turned slightly towards her, as though being led to a scene they did not wish to witness.

Matt picked his steps across the dizzying mosaic of graves, the spread of chemical green pebbles on one, giving way to golden flecks on the next. He moved briskly to catch up with the mourners. When he got there the man in front of him turned around, his shrunken, weather-battered face alive with curiosity. Deciding that Matt was a relation of Dixie's he offered his hand, said 'Sorry for your trouble,' stood back, and waited, until Matt agreed to go ahead of him.

Standing on one side of the grave among men, none of whom he recognized, Matt looked across at Madelene, puzzled by how unfamiliar and yet familiar she appeared. In an effort not to stare he looked down, examined his shoes noting how highly polished they were compared to those of the men on either side of him. When he raised his head Madelene was looking at him. He smiled, thinking he saw a flicker of recognition, but her expression remained unchanged.

Beside her, Rose and Statia appeared haggard. They had not merely given into old age, but welcomed its ravages, looking like streelish effigies of their former selves. Rose was wearing two coats, an age-streaked mackintosh over a bulky plaid. Several elaborate brooches, heavy costume pieces, hung loosely from the lapel of the raincoat. Her tightly cropped, alabaster-white hair, moulded to her head like plaster-of-Paris, exposed all the contours of her skull. But some stray impulse, a last-minute vanity, had prompted her to put on a marquisette hairband, a tiara of sorts, saving her from the inhuman fate of appearing like one of those shorn, feeble-minded women who roam the corridors of down-beat institutions for the aged. Statia was in full mourning garb, black hat, scarf and coat, all sabotaged by the gold-and-violet, sequinned evening bag she was clutching.

Mulling over their appearance, it occurred to Matt that they might be mocking the world, undermining its rites. Or maybe it was it was just a refusal to abandon glamour, to give up on those ideas which had coloured their lives with hope.

Still tightly linked to Madelene, they both shut their eyes and turned away as the coffin was lowered into the grave. Madelene leaned forward a little, followed its slow, even progress until it was eased onto the floor of the grave. Matt felt obliged to think about Dixie. But there wasn't a great deal to think about. He'd long since written him off as a feckless, hopelessly biddable character, a man guided through life by two sisters who were ill-equipped to do so. Still, his tightly-sprung, jerky voice, asking Matt to go down to the stream field that June afternoon all those years ago continued to mark the starting point of a journey from which he was inclined to shrink.

Some people were leaving the graveside, drifting over to the gate, their sombre pace, quickening as they approached it. Those who remained stood about waiting for an opportunity to sympathize with Statia and Rose. Madelene had her arms around them, directing their movements this way and that, handling them like precious antique dolls. Every so often they looked up at her, searched her face for an appraisal of their performance, which she provided by way of an indulgent smile. They then swung back into action, each holding a hand out in a random sort of way, waiting for it to be clasped. Matt too was waiting, obliged to make a move when the last remaining man at his side of the grave edged his way over to speak to them.

He watched out for a break in the flow of sympathizers. Rose and Statia were nodding in unison, attentive in a theatrical sort of way while a stooped woman in a lank fur coat whispered to them. When she went, Rose looked up and directly across at him. Steadied her head. She held her gaze, concentrating as though Matt couldn't be trusted to remain in her field of vision. Then, keeping him pilloried to the spot with her gaze, she began to tug at Madelene's coat sleeve, gently at first, soon vigorously, almost violently, for all the world a child desperate to get the attention of a parent. When Madelene looked over Matt was smiling. Smiling at Rose, at her, at the way things were unfolding. Just smiling.

He approached them, hand outstretched to Rose, unprepared for the fierceness of her grip. In that same instant Statia took his other hand, gripped it almost as tightly. Both turned to Madelene as though looking for guidance on how he ought to be greeted. Their perfume was sweet to the point of being acrid.

'I remember you.' Madelene's words were intoned with a mixture of surprise and assertion, underscored by a sense of achievement in being able to recall who Matt was. He smiled, thinking it was a joke, continuing to smile, though it was beginning to dawn on him that it wasn't. Those words, *I remember you*, were still rattling around in his head when he heard her announce, 'It's Matt Duggan.' She looked around, playfully commanding the attention of the loosely dispersing group. 'It's my Rathisland boyfriend. Fancy that.' She introduced him with a hand flourish. 'My Rathisland boyfriend,' she said again, making it sound like the refrain from a pop song.

She tipped her head towards Rose, then towards Statia, directing his attention to the welcome they were giving him.

Neither said a word. They positioned themselves directly in front of him, faces no more than a few inches from his, expressions fixed in questioning pouts. He wanted to disentangle but they remained there, transfixed, their bony hands resolutely clamping his, ghosts scrutinizing his face, searching for clues that might throw some light on the meaning of it all.

The instant Madelene spoke again they let go, left him with the sensation that he'd been unshackled, roughly dispatched before her for judgment.

'There's lunch in Dowlings. If you're not in a rush.'

'Why not? I'll slip in for a few minutes. Thanks. '

Someone from the small group behind him reached out and grasped Madelene's hand. Matt moved to the side, made room for an oldish, but fresh-faced man who, in a rapid burst of words, told Madelene he'd gone to school with Dixie. He clutched the hook of his walking stick with both hands, leaned forward, and in a series of rapidly drawn, short breaths, released a litany of praise for Dixie.

Rose and Statia were whispering to each other, their voices growing audible as they recalled this and that detail about someone who'd come to the funeral, a contemporary whom they hadn't seen since their youth. They talked in harmony, amending, disputing, revising, agreeing with such ease and precision that they might as well be speaking with the same voice.

'Musical. The piano. She played the piano. She did. Sang too. Can't say I ever heard her singing. A very talented pianist. Definitely. No, not a singer, not as far as I know. That was her aunt. Yes. She was the singer.'

Against the background of this rhythmic, time-perfected chorus Madelene's voice took on a loud, almost shrill tone.

'We better get going. The others will all be there …'

Matt wondered if her accent had always been so pointedly English.

The couple who had been sympathizing with Rose and Statia now turned their attention to Madelene, told her they were sorry for her trouble. The woman asked her when she was going back, to which Madelene replied, 'Early next week.' The man leaned towards her, assured her that if she needed a lift anywhere, to the train, or to the airport, he was available. Madelene told him Maurice, her son, who hadn't been able to make it to the funeral, was on his way over.

'I expect he'll hire a car at the airport,' she added, smiling broadly at the couple.

Matt sat in his car waiting for everyone to head off to Dowlings, before going back into the graveyard to look for Josef's grave. When, eventually, he located it, a long distance away from where he thought it was, he discovered from the finely sculpted marble plaque, that Josef's remains were no longer there. They had been removed and reburied in the German graveyard in Glencree, County Wicklow. Matt blessed himself, not as a prelude to prayer, but as an attempt at marking a moment he felt he ought to mark, before going back to his car.

Dowlings, he discovered as he drove up outside, was no longer called Dowlings, at least not officially. A faulty neon sign, competing with sharp bursts of December sunshine, intermittently illuminated its new name, The Rathisland Inn. The receptionist directed him to the 'upstairs room', to what she cheerily referred as the Coll function.

The stairwell smaller, pokier than he recalled, was still the gathering place for all the hotel's odours, a constantly changing cocktail of frying rashers, Harpic, cigarette smoke, laundry steam and stout. The low hum coming from the open door of the upstairs room broke into a mix of individual voices as he approached. He spotted Rose and Statia sitting at the edge of a wickerwork couch, each with a brimming sherry glass, thumb and two fingers pinching the stem. Their heads craned delicately towards the rims, eyes fluttering to a close as they prepared to sip. Madelene was close by, hurriedly taking off her coat. She smiled crisply when she saw Matt.

'Will you have something to drink?'

'Whiskey thanks, with a little water.'

Matt followed her over to the makeshift bar, a green, felt-topped table wedged into an alcove. The whiskey see-sawed in the glass as she turned around. A schoolboy waiter approached, asked her if he should get the sandwiches, snuffled, hiked up the waistband of his trousers with his wrists.

'I'm sure they're all here by now.' She surveyed the room as she spoke. 'I think we can go ahead.' Then turning her attention to Matt, tilted her glass forward a little. 'Cheers.'

Matt had lost almost all sense that the person in front of him was Madelene Coll, at least Madelene Coll as he had, until now, remembered her. Even her voice was unfamiliar. He wanted to say something, but there wasn't anything to say. He rolled the whiskey around in the glass, sipped a little, relieved when he saw that the manager, who had been taking people's coats at the door, was approaching them.

'Everything OK?' He surveyed the room, gestured to the waiter to move around with the sandwiches.

'Fine,' Madelene replied, smirking as she added, 'this is my Rathisland boyfriend, Matt Duggan.'

Matt laughed a little.

'Paddy Knowles,' the manager smiled, offered his hand, 'pleased to meet the Rathisland boyfriend.'

'I taught in the school here during the war. Madelene was an evacuee ...'

'An evacuee?' she exclaimed loudly, pronouncing each syllable separately, sneeringly inflecting the final one.

'Oh, come on,' she laughed, turned to the manager. 'My Dad was serving up north, in Scotland and what with his back turned and all, my Mum started carrying on.' She paused, looked at Matt in a challenging sort of way. 'Up the pole, wasn't she? Up the pole with my sister Min, when he came home on leave.' She laughed heartily.

Matt wondered if she somehow held him responsible for the fact that none of this had emerged all those years ago. He shrugged his shoulders, inadvertently prompting her to go on.

'His friend Ernie. She'd taken up with his friend Ernie. Hadn't she?'

'Some friend.' The manager laughed.

'Dad said he could have her,' Madelene laughed, 'said they could vamoose together.' She flung her hand out dramatically. 'And that's what they did, so I got sent to this place.' She grimaced. 'Back to his sisters.' She looked around the room, her face tightening, then slackening as she fixed on Statia and Rose.

'Must see to these people.' The manager held his hand up, twiddled his index finger in the direction of a group at the far side of the room.

'We were young, very young,' Matt smiled at Madelene, leaving his glass down on a nearby table. 'I must get going.' He edged his glass further in.

Madelene surveyed the crowd briefly before turning to him. 'It was …' she held out her hand, 'nice that you came.' There was a business-like thrust to their handshake, an unspoken agreement to allow each other hold onto the different versions of a story they'd once shared.

'I'll say goodbye to …' He nodded at Rose and Statia,

two silver-screen ancients, now thrown into disarray as Madelene, followed by Matt, approached. They started to rattle, jerk unpredictably like badly co-ordinated puppets, trying to make sure their sherry didn't spill. Madelene leaned down, explained slowly and loudly that Matt was going. The pace at which they were nodding accelerated. He backed away, held his hand up as he said goodbye, then quick-stepped his way across the room and down the stairs. The receptionist raised her head as he approached, tilted her chin, about to speak when her expression collapsed into childish curiosity.

He pulled out, bothered that his memory of his time in Rathisland had been uprooted by his return. Madelene, Rose and Statia, who'd occupied fixed positions in that memory for so long, had, in the course of the previous hour or so, been replaced by the people they'd now become. But before long these people began to merge into his memory of them. In that way they came to take their places in the larger world, their lives shaped on a stage, in which Matt, only one of many players, had had a brief walk-on part.

He thought of Canning, recalling the pomp with which he had officiated at his and Effie's marriage all those years back, his narrow head and big ears to the fore in the wedding photographs, an endless source of laughter for Emer and Carrie. He thought of Carmody and of other Carmodies he'd met since: thoughts that triggered a memory of browsing through the crates of second-hand books outside Greene's on Nassau Street and coming across a withered copy of *Dánta na hÉireann* in among a batch of redundant school textbooks. He examined the cover, an etching of the blind composer Ó Carolan poised to play his harp. He turned to the poem he'd read to the class that afternoon, Carmody's praise for his recital now laughable. And following in the wake of that memory, an image of himself browsing through the newspaper by the kitchen window in Willow Road, listening to Effie reading a large, colourfully illustrated edition of *Aesop's Fables* to Carrie and Emer, aged about five and three at the time. Towards the end of the story they leaned forward to look more closely at a detail to which Effie was drawing their attention. Their heads bunched in together over the book, then moved back in unison as they followed Effie's finger from the top to the bottom of the page.

'See. It's the cheese falling,' Effie said.

'See. It's the cheese falling,' Carrie repeated, jabbing the page with her finger.

When, a few moments later, Effie went upstairs to get their pyjamas, Carrie began to retell the story to Emer, running her finger under the lines, though at the time she couldn't read.

'There was a crow with a piece of cheese in its beak. There was a fox who wanted it. The crow was sitting on a branch high up in a big tree. The fox was down under the big tree.'

'See.' She caught Emer's hand and forcibly placed her index finger, first on the crow, then on the fox.

' "Give me the cheese," said the fox.

"No," said the crow. "I will not give you the cheese."

"If you will not give me the cheese, then will you sing for me?" ' She paused, hurriedly adding, ' "You have a beautiful voice."

"You have a beautiful voice," ' she said again, this time more emphatically, a springboard from which to leap to the end of the story.

'The crow opened his beak to sing and the cheese fell out. See. It fell out. Down onto the ground where the fox is gobbling it up.'

'I don't like cheese.' Emer announced, maybe assuring herself that the crow's loss wasn't as bad as Carrie was trying to make out. Matt laughed. They both looked in his direction, laughed too, their laughter becoming intermittent, then strangely distant.

Tell me. How did a city lad like you get so fluent? That's the finest Irish I've heard in this room since I came to this school. And that's neither today nor yesterday.

In the quiet of the kitchen that evening, a chunk of Rathisland, loosened by the fable of the Fox and the Crow, had fallen away, and, like the memories of Madelene, Rose and Statia with which he'd travelled to Rathisland that morning, had found its way into a larger well-charted world.